JMA SH⌊   ⌋WN

Before the com⌊   ⌋lroad, the only
way of mov⌊   ⌋the remote army
command ⌊   ⌋omesteads was by
riverboat ⌊   ⌋father killed under
mysteri⌊   ⌋ances, Mary Vender
s⌊   ⌋e 'verland Freighting
C⌊   ⌋froi ⌊   ⌋ma, in the face of
op⌊   ⌋the . 'v form 1, but
po⌊   ⌋naught orga 'is ⌊   ⌋that
war⌊   ⌋o all of the busin⌊   ⌋elf.
Not⌊   ⌋e tall stranger rode ⌊   ⌋n,
hi⌊   ⌋ru ⌊   ⌋ed down, the butts smc ⌊   ⌋d
po⌊   ⌋from long use, did there see⌊   ⌋y
hope ⌊   ⌋all for the struggling Over⌊   ⌋1
F1 ghting Company...

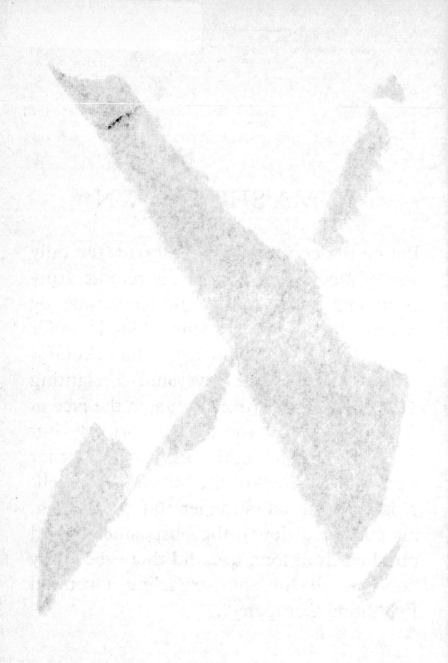

YUMA SHOWDOWN

YUMA SHOWDOWN

by

Seth Pemberton

Dales Large Print Books
Long Preston, North Yorkshire,
BD23 4ND, England.

British Library Cataloguing in Publication Data.

Pemberton, Seth
    Yuma showdown.

    A catalogue record of this book is
    available from the British Library

    ISBN   1-84262-331-1 pbk

First published in Great Britain in hardcover edition 2003
by Robert Hale Ltd.
Originally published in paperback as
Showdown at Yuma by Chuck Adams

Published in Large Print 2004 by arrangement with
Robert Hale Ltd.

Dales Large Print is an imprint of Library Magna Books Ltd.

Printed and bound in Great Britain by
T.J. (International) Ltd., Cornwall, PL28 8RW

00216374

1

OVERLAND TRAIL

The town was called Yuma, standing at the junction of the Colorado and Gila Rivers. To the north and east lay the great Arizona deserts while to the south, across the Mexico border, lay the Gulf of California. It was not a big town, but it had one claim to importance. It was here that the paddle-steamers ended their long haul up the river, unloading their supplies for the outlying Army posts and homesteads, many of them a hundred miles or more from the town.

For the rest of the way, the supplies had to be hauled across the desert by the great teams of Murphy wagons, the freighters, who operated out of Yuma to all points north and west.

Inside the saloon, fifty yards along the street from the quayside, the air was cool, blue with cigarette smoke and after the sun-blast of the dusty street outside, it made a welcome change to Matt Elston, wagonmaster of the Overland Freighting Company. Outside, in the street, the air packed a wallop that almost knocked a man down, bringing all of the moisture in his body boiling up to the surface. Too hot for work, and the wagons were not due in for another three hours or so.

Walking to the bar, he let his gaze flicker over the men already in the saloon. There were mostly men he knew, but three men stood against the bar, strangers to him. One was short, broad-built, rounded but not, Elston guessed, with fat. The man in the middle of the trio was, by comparison, tall and thin, his long sallow features bearing a look of mournful sombreness, brows seemingly drawn into a perpetual frown. The third was young, in his early twenties Elston reckoned, good-looking in a flashy sort of way, his outfit bright and gaudy, black hair just showing in tight curls beneath his sombrero, eyes as black as his hair with something dangerous smouldering in their depths. All three men carried hardware, low down on their hips like men who not only knew how to use a gun, but had used it often enough in the past to have made it a part of themselves.

Aston nodded to them as he took his place

at the bar. All three, glancing sideways, nodded back but there was no look of welcome on their features.

'Whisky,' he said to the bartender.

The other brought the bottle and a glass to him, pushed them forward over the counter. He seemed worried, kept glancing at the trio further along the bar.

'You expectin' the wagons this afternoon, Matt?'

'Should be rollin' in around four o'clock.' Elston lifted his glass, drank down a gulp of the raw spirits, felt it burn at the back of his throat, then tossed off the rest, setting the empty glass down in front of him.

There was a pause, then the tall thin man said harshly: 'You work for one of the freighting organisations in Yuma, mister?'

Elston turned, made a poker face at the other. The grey eyes that stared back at him on either side of the thin, pinched nose were flecked with green. Under the nose, there was a thin, pencil moustache and a gimlet mouth that was pressed into a tight line.

Elston cleared his throat. He had not intended to, just in case any of these men might figure him to be the nervous type, but it just came out. He made his voice soft and casual as he said: 'Sure. I work for Mary

Vender. She runs the Overland Freighting Company.'

The youngest of the three snickered briefly, lips twisted back from even, white teeth, and remarked 'Hear that, Faro. Seems like he's another of the boys who's backin' a loser here.'

'Maybe he don't know yet that the Overland is finished,' suggested the man called Faro. He spoke harshly without turning his head to glance in Elston's direction.

Elston stood quite still against the bar. He carried no gun, but wished that he had carried his bull-hide whip with him. Usually he had it looped around his belt, ready for use. Now he felt suddenly naked without it. He poured a second drink, lifted the glass, then paused as the short, stubby man edged swiftly along the bar, gripped his wrist and jerked sharply, the glass flying from Elston's hand and smashing to pieces on the floor behind him, the whisky trickling along the floor in a little pool.

'You heard what Cal said, mister,' he said, without raising his voice. 'We aim to run you and the Overland right out of this territory. You got anythin' to say to that?'

Elston turned his head sharply, squaring up to the other. For the first time, he noticed

12

the deep scar that ran diagonally along his cheek, twisting his mouth into a perpetual sneer. 'Seems to me that you're mighty free about thrown' other men's whisky around. Maybe you'd like to pay for the next drink?'

The other uttered a harsh bark of laughter. Behind him, Cal grinned bleakly, his eyes brooding. 'Guess you'd better work him over,' he said casually, 'just to teach him manners. Sooner he learns that around here any *hombre* who doesn't carry a shootin' iron had better not speak out of turn, the easier it'll be for him in the end.'

'Let me do it, Faro,' said the young one, pushing himself smoothly away from the bar. His spurs rattled as he moved lithely forward, arms swinging a little by his sides.

Faro moved away, nodding. But he did not go far, stopping close enough to back the other's play if anything went wrong. Elston turned away from the bar. He knew from the look of him that this man would be a dirty fighter.

'Just teach him to mind his manners, Torro,' said Cal, watching the proceedings through the long mirror behind the bar. 'We don't want any trouble with the sheriff here; not just yet.'

Torro chuckled softly. Stepping forward

13

he tried to crowd Elston against the bar, swung with his left hand, but the Overland wagonmaster side-stepped and made him miss. Elston knew that with this *hombre* there would be no more talking. He had worked himself up into a fight, his black eyes shining with hunger and he knew he had to do something fast, without waiting. Even as Torro stumbled a little, caught off balance by the bigger man's move, Elston caught him by the arm, swung him round and slammed a fist at the other's face. Blood spurted from the smashed cartilage of his nose, streaking his once-handsome features. For a moment his mouth puckered like a baby whose bottle had been snatched away from it. He wiped his hand over his face, stared down at the blood which streaked the back of it, then glanced up with amazement that anything could have happened to him. Elston shifted, jabbed at the other's face again, his fist grazing along the cheek. Torro went back hard against the bar, his shoulders striking it with an impact that shook the bottles arranged on top of it. He started to go down, his mouth working, but somehow he held himself up and shook his head, clearing it, spitting blood from his mouth. Elston was on him again. He feinted and jabbed, his fist landing solidly on the other's chest, then the left and the right again, each blow landing with a savage force, now the stomach and then a cross to the jaw as the other's guard dropped. Torro was cowering, hunching his shoulders, bobbing and weaving slowly. But suddenly he moved, swinging a haymaker up from his boots. It caught Elston unprepared on the forehead, stunning him, sending him reeling back into one of the tables that collapsed under his weight, sending him sprawling on the floor, the wood splintering under him.

Torro seized his chance, bored in, lifting his right foot to bring it down hard on Elston's chest. His lips were drawn back from his bloodied mouth in a snarling, bestial grin, his black eyes alight with an evil triumph. The long, Spanish-looking spurs seemed larger than life as they came stamping down. For what seemed an eternity, Elston lay there, staring up at that descending boot, knowing that when it landed, it would crush his chest, fracture his ribs.

The boot grew bigger and bigger while Elston lay there wondering what to do about it. It seemed as though he was nailed there to the floor with a strip of wood from the broken table sticking painfully into the small of his back. Then, at the very last moment, he found himself able to move. Jerking up his arms, he caught hold of the other's ankle, twisted violently. The edge of the spurs ripped the flesh on the palm of his left hand, drawing the blood, but he scarcely noticed this. Torro flailed his arms as he tried to keep his balance, uttered a high-pitched yell of anger and went over sideways, crashing against the side of the bar, knocking his head against the solid wood.

It took every last ounce of strength that Elston had in his body to heave himself on to his feet and dive on top of the other, fingers reaching out for the man's throat, tightening around it as he bore down with all of his weight. Torro's thumbs went for his eyes, struggling to gouge them from their sockets and he was forced to rear his head back in an attempt to break free of them. Anger gave him strength. Lifting the other's head, he slammed it down hard on to the floor, repeated the move, made to do it for a third time when he grew aware that Faro had stepped forward to intervene in the fight. The other had his Colt in his hand, the weapon reversed. Aiming it for the back of Elston's head, he swung.

There was no time for the other to avoid

16

the blow altogether. Jerking his head instinctively to one side, he managed to ride it a little, the butt of the gun catching him on the side of the skull. He sagged on top of Torro. With an oath, the other pushed him off, hauled himself to his feet, holding on to the edge of the bar to stop himself falling again. His features were twisted into a livid snarl of hate. For a second, he glared down at Elston's form, then drew back his foot and kicked him hard in the kidneys. The agony that lanced through the wagon-master's body somehow had the effect of jerking him back to full awareness. He sucked in a sharp gasp of pain, squirmed as he saw the booted foot swinging in again for another kick. This time it landed on the back of his left shoulder, numbing his arm all the way to his fingertips.

Thrusting the Colt back into its holster, Faro dragged Elston upright, pinning his arms behind him. At the bar, Cal said harshly, 'What in hell you playin' at, Torro? You figurin' on lettin' him finish you instead?'

Torro did not answer him directly. Instead, he looked murderously at Elston, held in Faro's grip. 'Just you hold him there,' he said, sucking in great gasps of air.

'He marked me. Goddamn, I aim to see that he don't forget this. Ain't nobody marked Torro Mendez before.'

'You're big and brave just so long as you've got somebody holdin' down your opponent,' Elston sneered at him.

Torro went red around the collar. He brushed the back of his hand over his nose and mouth, then moved in, still catlike on his feet. His fists ripped and slashed, catching Elston from all angles. He continued to beat and pummel as the wagonmaster struggled in vain to break free of the stocky man's iron-like grip. As he felt his senses leave him, he lifted his foot, kicked savagely at Torro as the other moved in, confident that he had his man at his mercy. His boot caught the other high on the thigh, sending him staggering back, uttering a thin bleat of agony.

'So you want to play, do you, son-of-a-bitch,' grunted Torro, straightening up with an effort which cost him a lot. He hopped around on his sound foot for a moment, glancing in the direction of the bar, then said sharply: 'Cal!'

The bartender had bent to reach for the scattergun he kept in a convenient place under the counter, ready for use at a time such as this. He froze at once as Cal thrust

18

his Colt over the bar, levelling it on the other's chest.

'Freeze right there, mister,' he said ominously. 'We aim to finish our business with this *hombre* without any interference from you. Now back off or I'll blow a hole through your middle.'

The bartender hesitated for a moment, then shrugged. One look into the bleak eyes told him that the other would not stop to implement his threat. He had faced up to several hotbloods in the past, but this man was different.

'All right, Torro,' Cal called. 'Go ahead and when you've finished with him, drag him out and dump him in the alley. But be quick about it. We don't want the law here or there'll be trouble with Quentin.'

Torro came forward again, more warily this time, knuckled his fists and swung savagely, with no reason behind his punches, only wanting to make his man suffer before he blacked out completely. Elston slumped in Faro's arms. There was the salty taste of blood in his mouth and his lips felt as though they were swollen to twice their normal size. His chest hurt like fire where the hard fists kept pounding at his bruised ribs. His head rang and there was a shimmering red haze in front of his vision. He knew that he was in for a real beating now and yet the only thing that worried him, that made him angry, was the knowledge that he could do nothing to fight back, could not touch the grinning, sneering face that wavered in front of him.

When he came round, he was lying in a huddled heap in the hot, grey dust in the alley. The way he was feeling, he was so bagged up that he could not move for several minutes. The sunlight was a glaring pain in his eyes, bringing a throbbing ache to his forehead like a hammer going in his skull. Dried blood had congealed around his nose and mouth and there was a foul taste there which he failed to get rid of as he spat some of the dust and blood from between his torn lips.

Very gently, he explored his body. His chest ached intolerably. It felt as if every rib had been busted inside him. Each breath he dragged down into his tortured lungs blistered like fire with stabs of agony lancing through his body. But there did not seem to be anything broken. Slowly, he peeled himself off the ground, leaned against the sun-baked wall, trembling, head swelling like a balloon with every pulse-beat of his heart.

Legs as limp as boiled rhubarb, he hauled himself to his feet and attempted to dust some of the dirt from his clothing. The sick, muzzy feeling in the bottom of his stomach made him want to retch and he was forced to lean against the wall with his head hanging down between his arms for long moments before he could summon up enough strength to move along the alley and out into the sunblasted length of the main street. Staggering drunkenly from side to side, he made his way along towards the quay, scarcely aware of what he was doing.

A man came forward, caught him by the arm, held him up, staring into his face. Elston did not recognise the other's features, nor his voice as he said: 'You all right, friend? Want me to help you to a doctor?'

'I'll make out,' Elston said. The words were a hoarse mumble through his lips and he had to push them out so they sounded strange, the voice utterly unlike his own. His hands were shaking as much as his legs, but he managed to push the other's hand away. 'Don't worry about me, mister. I'll remember this when the time comes.'

Watching him, the man chewed reflectively on his cigar end, then shrugged and turned away. Stumbling, Elston made his way along the fronts of the tall, imposing buildings, the stores, granaries and hotels, until he reached the tall, wooden gates across which were the words: OVERLAND FREIGHTING COMPANY in faded gilt paint.

They were half open and he pushed his way inside, walked over the wide courtyard, up the steps to the office. He almost fell to his knees as he went inside, managed to catch himself, drew in a couple of deep breaths. They hurt his chest, but it made him feel a little better inside his skull. The meek-looking man seated behind the mahogany desk at one side of the office looked round sharply, then got nervously to his feet, moved forward hesitantly.

'Matt. What happened, man?' He caught Elston under one arm, struggled to hold the other up as the wagonmaster felt the strength drain from him once more. Vaguely, Elston was aware of Carmody calling urgently, of another door opening. Then Mary Vender had come into the office, had him by the other arm and they were helping him to a chair, sitting him in it and holding him there while he struggled to keep a tight grip on his reeling senses.

'Who did this to you, Matt?' There was a sharp note in Mary's voice.

'Three *hombres* in the saloon,' he muttered thickly. 'Started a fight soon as they heard who I was workin' for. They said somethin' about the Overland bein' finished, somethin' about the wagons not gettin' through today.'

'And they beat you up for that?'

'Weren't no other reason for 'em to do it. I was just drinkin' peaceful and then they started. Phil, the bartender tried to stop it, but they held a gun on him.'

Mary went to the window, looked out, a frown creasing her face. She stood there for a long moment, then said in a hushed voice: 'This is only the beginning of what I've been afraid of for some time, Matt. I guessed it was coming when my father died.'

'You still think your father was murdered?' With an effort, Elston lifted his head and stared at her, blinking his eyes in the sunlight that streamed through the window. He rubbed the back of his hand over his mouth, fingered the bruised lips carefully.

'Don't you?' she countered, turning to face him. There was a steely look in the level grey eyes. 'Somebody wanted him dead so they could take over the Overland. He always refused to sell out. So he had to be got rid of. Then they thought it would be easier to browbeat me and get me to sell. Now they've obviously discovered that isn't so, and they've decided to move in and start by causing trouble. Then there'll be attempts to stop the wagons, make us lose our contracts with the military and the homesteaders.'

Elston nodded his head slowly. 'There was some talk in the saloon about me backing the losin' side,' he murmured. 'I didn't think much of it then, but it sure makes sense now.'

'Next they'll start to carry freight at cut-throat rates so as to make it impossible for us to carry on.'

'There's that big organisation that's just started up along the street, Miss Mary,' said Carmody quietly.

'You talkin' about the Connaught organisation?' Elston said harshly. He sat up a little straighter in his chair.

'That's the one, I reckon. All of the others are small fry, smaller than we are and they've been operatin' out of Yuma for as long as the Overland. They wouldn't try to horn in and grab off the lot.'

Mary hesitated, then moved back into the middle of the room, her hands twisted in her lap. 'He's right, Matt,' she said softly, seriously. 'It has to be the Connaught organisation that's behind all of this. I know when they started up in Yuma, they tried to buy my father out but he always resisted, said that if there was only one freighting organisation it would be the worst possible thing for the territory. It would mean that one man would be able to charge any rates he liked because there'd be no opposition. He'd have a stranglehold on the military and the homesteaders who rely on us to bring in their supplies from the river steamers.'

'Who runs the Connaught?' Matt asked tightly.

'Man by the name of Earl Quentin,' Carmody said, going back to his desk. 'He's out of town right now. Due back in a few days time.'

'Quentin,' said Elston. 'That makes sense. Those three gunslingers in the saloon said they didn't want any trouble for Quentin. They must be workin' for him.'

'That's more than likely,' said the girl. 'But this isn't the worst. We still have our contracts and if we can fight Quentin's men, we have a chance of holding on to them. The people around here trust us and so long as we can get through with the supplies, I think they'll stick with us.'

'So what's the worst?' Elston asked. He

pushed himself to his feet, straightened up with an effort.

'There's talk that Quentin has sent out of town for a gunman to do his dirty work for him. Some gunhawk from Eastern Arizona named the Morenci Kid.'

'The Morenci Kid,' Elston repeated dully. 'Seems like I've heard that name before. A bad *hombre* to tangle with. Plenty of tales told about him. Pretty near as poisonous a gunslinger as Billy the Kid or Wyatt Earp. But I never figured he'd be brought in here.'

'That's the talk which is going around town anyway,' said Mary Vender. 'If it's true, then I doubt if we shall be in business here much longer. I can fight men like Quentin. I can do my best to meet even the cut-throat rates he might try to force me out of the freighting business, but when it comes to gunplay, then I want nothing of it.'

'Your pa built up this freighting line by fighting for what he thought was right,' Elston said tersely. 'If you think it's worth hangin' on to, then you'll have to go on fightin', just as he did.'

'We can't fight men like the Morenci Kid,' Mary said harshly, shaking her head. 'Use sense, Matt! We can't hire gunmen of that breed and if we did, it would only mean the start of a war around Yuma that would destroy us all. No, I want no part of that.'

'Anyone know when this gunslinger is due to hit town?'

'Only that he'll arrive in the next few days. He may come back with Quentin.'

'I'll keep my eyes open for any stranger arrivin' in town,' Elston promised.

Mary glanced out of the window once more, then said a trifle sharply, 'I'd prefer it if you'd ride out along the trail a little way, Matt; check on those wagons. If what you heard in the saloon was true, there may be trouble and they won't be expecting it.'

With the blazing disc of the sun still close to the zenith, throwing only short shadows over the yellow-white desert, the tired oxen hauled, bawling, on the traces, dragging the wagons through the ankle-deep dust of the trail. There was little water left in the barrels slung under the huge Murphy wagons and the men who rode on the high tongues, or in the saddle beside the creaking wagons, were sickened and stunned by the endless glare. There had been long, sun-filled days and short, cold nights on the trail. Tempers were short, flared often. Men itched with impatience to see the end of the trail, to sight the pale grey smudge on the eastern horizon that was Yuma. The mere thought of it made the mouth water. Cool beer, whisky in the saloons, real fresh food, well cooked in the eating houses along the streets that fronted the quayside. Even the thought of all that water that flowed endlessly along the Colorado River haunted men's dreams during the bitter cold of the nights, with their tongues rusted against the roofs of their parched mouths and throats painfully constricted by thirst.

Now they were on the last day of the drive back to Yuma. By nightfall, they should have reached the town. There would be pay waiting for them and the chance to spend the golden dollars on food and drink.

Seated on the tongue of the lead wagon, Jeb Kirby shaded his eyes with his hand and stared out at the ridges of sand and dust with the trail running arrow-straight through them. He shifted positions as his body cramped and he rolled and smoked cigarettes to pass the time, but the smoke only served to increase the thirst in his dried-out throat. He studied the terrain which still lay ahead of them thoughtfully, turned as one of the outriders came alongside the wagon, pushed back the sombrero on to the back of his head, wiped the sweat from his forehead.

'Hell, but I'll be glad when we can leave this dust and heat and wagons behind. Another ten miles and this trip will be behind us and we can–'

A rifle shot cracked the clinging heat-filled stillness and echoed thinly in the wide canyon that opened ahead of them, the walls of which rose smoothly from the flatness of the scorched desert. Then another shot and another, and tiny puffs of dirt lifted from the sides of the trail around the line of wagons. Kirby yelled a warning, heard the leaden smack of a slug against the wooden post within a couple of inches of his head, Jerking hard on the reins, he hauled the four oxen to a slithering halt in the treacherous sand, wound the reins tightly around the post and grabbed for the Springfield. Behind him, the rest of the wagons had stopped. Another flurry of shots before the riders had swung around the train, jerking the rifles from their leather scabbards, moving their horses to return the fire.

'Look!' One of the men yelled the warning harshly, pointing a hand. The cloud of dust was ominous. The tightly-knit bunch of riders were spurring their horses forward at a cruel, punishing pace. Kneeling against the tongue on which he had been sitting a few moments earlier, Kirby sighted along the Springfield, caught the head and shoulders of one of the riders in the notch of the sights and squeezed the trigger. The man jerked in the saddle, slipped sideways, then toppled to the dirt, one leg caught in the stirrup, the plunging horse, spooked by the sudden roar of gunfire, dragging him beside it through the white dust.

The attackers were so desperate to get their job done with that they had thrown caution to the winds, or perhaps they had not figured on meeting the heavy and accurate return fire from the wagon train. Several saddles were emptied as they stormed past a hundred yards or so away, firing as they rode. But the fire from the men hidden among the rocks along the sides of the canyon had increased too and several men among the wagons had fallen.

Ignoring the gunfire for a moment, Kirby lifted himself up to his full height and stared back along the train. He realised at once that unless they met this attack with cunning, they would all be lost. At the top of his lungs, he yelled: 'Swing the wagons around and stay under cover!'

Whipping the teams of oxen, the drivers

struggled to bring the cumbersome wagons around so that they might face any direction of attack. It was an old manoeuvre, harking back to the days of the pioneers, but it was still the best method of defence in circumstances such as these. Slugs chopped into the woodwork of the wagons, slicing through the canvas. Crouching down behind the uprights, Kirby stared through the swirling dust and gunsmoke which hid many of the enemy from view. He was at a loss to understand this unprovoked assault on them. His first thought that the Indians had gone on the warpath unknown to them was soon rejected. These men were not Indians. Yet they were fighting with the cunning of the red man.

The men on horseback had warily withdrawn into the distance rather than risk any more of their number, leaving the gunfire to the men among the rocks. The hot day was alive with the deafening racket of the guns. Bullets shrieked and whined in murderous ricochet off metal and stone. Splinters of wood lanced past his head as he fired at any target that showed itself.

A head showed itself momentarily in a vee among the rocks high up on the left-hand slope. Kirby caught the abrupt movement at the very edge of his vision, jerked his head around, reloaded the Springfield, waited patiently. His eyes were fixed on the spot where he knew the other to be. When the head lifted cautiously again, he had the weapon sighted on the place. The sound of the shot and the jerk of the rifle against his wrist seemed to come in the same instant. The head vanished and a second later, a body hurtled down the slope, bouncing from one rocky outcrop to another until it hit the floor of the canyon like a limp sack of grain and lay still.

More gunfire broke. Bullets rattled and rustled about the wagons, but by now most of the men were under cover, out of reach of the searching lead. For all the harsh, scorching blaze of the day, Kirby felt a chill on his flesh and a shiver moved up and down his spine. There was something wrong here, something he could not even begin to understand. The freight wagons had been allowed to move through this stretch of territory unhampered, unmolested. The Army had protected them in the beginning when the Indians were hostile. But all of that had been more than fifteen years before. Now there was peace here and everyone was trying to build up the towns of the frontier, open up the trails. Until the railroads were pushed as far west as this – and at the moment there was talk of them having only reached Abilene – the freight lines were the only means of getting goods and supplies from one place to another. So why should anyone attack them in this way? It was a problem he could not answer; and one for which there was now no time to seek an answer. There was time only in which to act instinctively and try to keep alive. Whoever those men were out there, they wanted him and the others dead. This wasn't just an attack to scare them off. Total destruction was the aim behind the ambush.

There came a long silence, broken only by a solitary gunshot. A crawling figure moved alongside the wagon, caught at the edge of the tongue, fingers gripping it with a wiry strength and slowly, the man pulled himself up as Jeb grabbed at his arm, helping him while still keeping an eye on the crowd of men in the distance. They seemed on the point of coming in again.

'How bad you hurt, Shorty?' Jeb asked, glancing at the deep stain on the other's sleeve. There was more blood on his shirt where he had been shot through the shoulder. 'We'd better get those wounds tied up.'

'Not a chance of that right now, Jeb.' The other shook his head, went on grimly: 'They're all around us now. We can't move from here without runnin' into a hail of bullets. Suppose they decide to rush us just as you're tryin' to tie it up? It ain't all that bad – it'll do until we get out of this mess, if we ever do get out. That crowd mean business.'

'You recognise any of 'em when they rushed us the last time?'

'Nope. Never seen any of 'em before. What you reckon they're after?'

'Can't be anythin' we're carryin' in the wagons. They must know, whoever they are, that we come back empty. We don't even pick up any money on the return journey.'

'So they must be just out to smash the wagons,' said Shorty hopelessly. He moved a little, sliding down into the back of the wagon as more gunfire broke out and bullets chirruped softly through the air around them. His face was twisted into a grimace of agony as the movement jarred his shoulder. Fresh blood oozed from the wound and soaked into his shirt.

Jeb nodded. He scrutinised the rocky walls of the canyon where the hidden riflemen lurked but could distinguish no sign of them. However, he knew they were still there, having the open stretch of ground still in view, waiting for the men on horseback to drive them forward in a desperate attempt to escape, to break through the ring of weapons that had been carefully forged around them, when they would inevitably shoot them down with an expert precision.

'It's my guess that these *hombres* have been paid by somebody, probably in Yuma, to destroy the wagons. I'll wager it could be the doin' of that new outfit that started up there a little while ago. From what I heard, the man who runs it has boasted he'll take over every other outfit in town before three months are out.'

Shorty's lips formed into an expression of dismay. He had joined up with the team only a little while before, was still new to the tough game of freighting. His voice rose a little in pitch, some of it occasioned by the pain that racked his body, some by the fear that had lifted in his mind. 'You mean to say, Jeb, that they also aim to kill us, too.' He shook his head slowly in vague disbelief. 'But for God's sake, we ain't been takin' any sides in anythin' that's been goin' on between the Connaught and Miss Vender. We just collect our wages at the end of each drive and that's all there is to it.'

Jeb answered tightly: 'That ain't quite all there is to it, Shorty. You'll soon find out that out here there's still very little law and order around. In Yuma maybe everythin' is done accordin' to the law. But not way out here in the desert. You know Earl Quentin's kind. He don't make any boast unless he's got the men and the guns to back it up.'

He rolled on to his side for a moment, stared up at the vivid blue-white of the early afternoon heavens that stretched in a vast inverted bowl over their heads, ablaze with the fiery light and heat of the Arizona sun. Still plenty of hours left to sundown. Even then, if they managed to hold out that long, there might be little chance of slipping through this ambush and into Yuma. A few zapilote buzzards circled like tattered pieces of black cloth against the cloudless sky, wheeling in lazy, patient circles beneath the sun, waiting for their chance to move in; the scavengers of the desert.

Shorty's face had grown paler with every second, as he digested what Jeb had said. He gulped, swallowed thickly. He saw what was coming, knew that unless a miracle happened, his life might be drawing rapidly to a close, that it could come by either a bullet or a rope, depending on how these killers felt when they got to him and he knew in his own heart that he had done nothing whatever to deserve such an end, for life to have dealt him such a raw deal. The realisation was so bitter that he could taste it in his mouth. He laid his face against the hot metal of one of the stanchions, felt it burn into his flesh, but lacked the necessary strength or desire to move. In front of him, the smooth barrel of the Springfield glimmered bluely in the sunlight, the flashes of reflected light jarring painfully into his eyes.

Jeb glanced at him out of the edge of his vision. He could guess at what the other was thinking at that moment, felt a little like that, too. Jeb had, unlike Shorty Weston, led a stormy and sometimes lawless life. He had often been forced to look death squarely in the face, had felt the wind of the man with the scythe close to him on numerous occasions. But this was the first time he felt really afraid. Through the shimmering haze, he watched the line of men on horseback anxiously. No shot had been fired at that for some minutes now and a little hope was beginning to filter back into his mind. Maybe once the wagons failed to turn up in Yuma on time, Mary Vender would send out some of the boys to see what had happened.

But that wouldn't come for some time yet. An hour overdue would not be looked upon as anything out of the ordinary. A busted wheel could delay them by that much time. Doubtless she would wait until nightfall before sending anyone out to look for them and judging by the determination of these killers, that would be far too late. Well, it was probably too late now. They were deep in the mire and it would need something more than sheer guts and good luck to drag them out of it.

Shorty was in severe pain now, lying with his head against the burning metal. He fingered his smashed shoulder gingerly, judged that the slug must have gone all the way through without touching the bone, but he had inevitably lost a lot of blood and he was feeling dizzy, had to blink his eyes several times as the desert tilted in front of his vision.

'Here they come again.' Jeb's words snapped him sharply back to the present. Weakly, he reached out for the Springfield, levered a cartridge into the breech and steadied himself on his side, forcing his vision through the haze of pain.

The men rode forward. Jeb tensed himself, waiting for the gunfire, but it did not come, instead there was something far more deadly. The men had evidently been prepared for anything. The storm of arrows that came whistling through the air were tipped with flame and smoke. It was an old Indian trick, used against the men in the wagons. Ripping through the cloth and canvas, thudding into the woodwork, dry as timber from the long exposure to the hot Arizona sun, the flames caught and licked about three of the wagons in as many seconds. Men struggled to beat out the flames, exposing themselves recklessly to the gunfire that rattled from among the rocks. It was a well executed move.

Jeb grabbed at the shaft of one arrow, sticking into the tongue of the wagon, jerked it free, regardless of the burning, blistering heat of it on his hands. He tossed it away into the dust, caught up his Springfield and levered half a dozen shots into the milling men, felt a sense of satisfaction as two of them dropped from their saddles and fell, inert, on to the ground, their horses galloping riderless away into the distance.

Turning his head, he peered at the wagon immediately behind him. Smoke, thick and laced with flame, was boiling up from it as the fire consumed it swiftly. Spreading, remorseless, the flames caught at the wounded man who dragged himself from the interior, still clutching his rifle. Inching out on to the long tongue, the other reached the edge, dropped on to the dust and rolled over and over, threshing wildly as the flames licked at his clothing. The man dropped his gun, grabbed at the ground with futile, fluttering fingers, dragging his useless legs behind him, the mere movement adding fuel to the flames that enveloped him, feeding on the cloth of his shirt and trousers. A high, thin scream of rage and pain was torn from the figure, unending, an intolerable sound that sent spasms trembling along nerves already stretched to breaking pitch, a scream which was strangled at last into a horrible, rasping gurgle which ended abruptly as the cartridge belt around his middle began to explode in a series of detonations.

Sickened, Jeb turned his head away. Anger laced through his body and mind. He threw a swift glance towards the trail which ran through the canyon, reached a sudden decision. The group of horsemen, those still in the saddle, were riding slowly back to the entrance of the canyon. Evidently they had decided to join their companions in the rocks where they would be able to find plenty of cover.

'Everybody into the wagons,' he yelled at the top of his voice. 'We'll ride 'em down. Keep under cover as much as possible!'

They were under fire before they reached the end of the canyon. Ahead of them, through the cloud of dust which partially obscured the riders, Jeb saw the faint flashes of the rifles from the marksmen among the rocks, heard the whining hum of the bullets slicing through the air. But there was no turning back now. The die was cast. Twenty yards to go and he could make out the milling bunch of riders, could see the grey, dust-streaked faces as they lifted their heads and saw death rushing at them in the form of the great oxen, now almost stampeding through the canyon.

He crouched low down, almost kneeling on the wagon tongue, grasping the thick leather reins tightly in his hands, Shorty lying beside him, his head buried in his hands. Rifles cracked from the rocks in an irregular volley. Then the tons of beef and muscle that were the straining, heaving oxen, smashed into the line of men. Screams rose as the horses went down in the face of the stampeding run. There was no escape for the riders. Hurled from their saddles they were either flung savagely against the base of the rocky walls or trampled underfoot as the wagons passed over them.

Somehow, Shorty thrust himself up on to one knee, gripping his Colt in a shaking hand. He fired at a man who sat tall in the saddle, a man who was miraculously un-harmed as the wagon train streamed past him. The shot took the other full in the chest, pitching him sideways in the saddle. Out of the corner of his eye, Jeb saw the stunned look of stupefied amazement on the gun-man's face. Then they were past him and the man was lost behind them, obliterated by the great cloud of dust lifted by the plunging hooves of the oxen and the churning wheels of the huge Murphy wagons.

Sucking in great breaths in an attempt to relieve the dry, racking torment in his chest, Jeb guided the wagon team through the pass, out into the open ground which lay beyond, stretching clear to Yuma. They were well clear now, thinned by the gunfire and with at least four wagons left behind, burning wrecks on the far side of the canyon.

The staccato crackle of gunfire dwindled into the distance behind them, but he still kept up the punishing pace until he was certain there would be no pursuit. Flung-up dust was a silver screen through which he saw details of the trail. Behind him, the remaining wagons thundered their way forward, wheels and braces creaking ominously. The oxen strained in the traces, bellowing angrily as they were forced to exert themselves still more after the long journey.

They passed through a short stand of timber where long, straggling branches hung low over the trail, turned downgrade again before swinging out into the flatness of the narrow belt of desert close to Yuma. Tall buttes, huge columns of red sandstone etched and fluted into fantastic shapes and contours lifted sheer from the dust.

Far off, to the north-west, the long chain of high mountains lifted a purple-hazed outline to the glaring sky, rising like a barrier across the horizon. They were tall and inaccessible and few men knew, or cared, what their rugged fastnesses concealed. This part of the territory was still sparsely populated. This was the lawless frontier of the United States, empty and barren and not kindly towards Man. Life was hard and tough for anyone who came to these parts and only the strong and the utterly ruthless, could survive here.

They were less than half a mile from Yuma when they met Matt Elston, spurring his mount towards them, a plume of white dust stretching out behind him. Concern and alarm showed on the wagonmaster's face as he surveyed the wagons in the team. He reined up beside Jeb as the other hauled the team to a halt.

'Goddamn, Jeb! What happened?'

Jeb gave him a bright-black stare. His voice was hard. 'Some bunch of killers jumped us back there. Shot up the whole train. We lost three or four wagons, set 'em on fire with fire-arrows.'

'Indians?' There was a note of incredulous amazement in Elston's voice.

'Nope.' Jeb took out a thick wad of tobacco, wrenched off a mouthful with a pull of powerful teeth, began to chew on it slowly. 'They was no Indians, though they used the same sort of dirty tricks.'

There was a delay, then Elston said: 'Better get movin', Jeb. Miss Vender is waitin' at the depot. She'll talk to you there. We figured somethin' like this might happen, that's why I rode out to take a look-see for myself.'

'Seems a pity nobody told us. We might've been able to give a better account of ourselves if we'd known. What is it? Some kind of range war that flared up all of a sudden?'

'Worse than that.' Elston jerked his

44

mount's head around with a savage twist of the reins. 'The Connaught organisation is tryin' to take over all of the freighting lines running out of Yuma. They've already started with some of the smaller ones, buyin' those up who'll sell at half their worth, runnin' the others out of business.'

'And now it's to be our turn.'

'Looks as if they really mean business.' Elston jerked a thumb at Shorty, lying behind Jeb. 'How bad is he hurt?'

'Bullet in the arm and another through the shoulder. He'll pull through if I get him to Doc Harding before he loses a sight more blood. But we lost some good men in that gunfight.' He said nothing more after that, but lashed the oxen with the long whip as if venting a little of his burning anger on them.

2

SIXGUN FOR SALE

Wayne Everett left the wide trail soon after quitting Los Lobos. Judging from the look of the country that lay to the west in the direction of the Gila River, there was more than a good chance of being jumped by any of the local badmen who might be on the look out for any strangers riding into this part of the territory. Not that he was really anticipating any bad trouble. Since leaving Tucson, further to the east, he had encountered very few other riders on this trail. But even though the hunch might turn out to be a poor one, it was one he meant to play until something happened to show him up wrong.

It had been early dawn when he had saddled up and left the small town and then the air had been clear and blue and cool. Now the sun was up at his back, throwing his long, black shadow almost directly in front of him, and already there was the feel and the smell of heat in the air. Out here, along the great deserts of Arizona, it was possible to smell the beginnings of the heat. It was an acrid scent compounded of dust and dried-out vegetation, or scorched, sun-baked earth that had never known a man's hand to a plough, possibly never would, and the cooler hills were always mere vaguely-seen purple shadows in a haze of dust-devils along the distant skyline.

Away from the trail which here was little more than a beaten track through an otherwise trackless waste, the land was uneven and a tawny yellow in colour. He sighted an occasional purple lizard that skitted from one concealing shadow to another whenever he approached close enough to disturb it and once, there came the warning rattle among the rocks and a sinuous shape slid almost in front of his mount. He calmed the animal swiftly, leaning forward over the horse's neck, speaking in a low, soothing tone to it. Fortunately, the animal was not a temperamental beast, otherwise it might easily have been spooked by the rattler.

Scoured flat by the desert winds, studded here and there by flat-topped sanded rooks, the bare flats lay between the tall amber bluffs and off to his right, looming huge and high, a mesa stood out from its background forming a wide barrier that stood against the blue heavens in a wide wall of rock.

He sat hunched forward a little in the saddle to make it easier on the horse. There was still quite a way to ride and through the worst part of the day, while back in Los Lobos, he had been told that there was little, if any, water along this route during the drought period of the year. There had also been that veiled warning of men who lurked among the tumbled rocks, waiting to pick off an unwary traveller with a bullet in the back, of men who had been shot down in this way for only a handful of dollar bills in their pockets, their bodies left to rot, or for the zapilote buzzards who always seemed to frequent these flats.

Cactus was plentiful, straight and thin, tall spiny growths of a dark brown-green colour that rustled dryly in the breeze, talking in ominous whispering tones among themselves, like an army of silent men, watching every move he made. It gave him a creepy feeling and he found his gaze flickering from one side of his route to the other. Sage and chamisa dotted the ground between the cacti, but for the most part, the desert was barren and empty, sucked dry of every drop of moisture by the white sun that glared down with a savage wickedness over everything as if determined to leave the ground dead of thirst.

He rode forward with caution, knowing that he could be seen for miles by the dust cloud he left behind him, that he made a perfect target over a distance of a good quarter of a mile for a man with a high-powered rifle. Keeping the trail in sight, he dipped into shallow gullies, his mount pussy-footing it over the bare stretches of rock, its hoofbeats muffled whenever it hit the sand again. The breeze increased a little as the morning wore on, began to whip up the yellow sand, tearing it loose from the crests of the dunes, sending it beating against his face. He pulled off his kerchief, knotted it around his mouth, keeping out most of the irritating grains which sought entry into his lungs.

High noon and the heat head had reached the top of its piled-up intensity. Sweat trickled down the lines of his cheeks and mingled with the dust into an itching mask. He knew better than to rub it. The merest touch could abrade the flesh into a raw, bleeding mass. He would just have to bear it until he reached Yuma.

There were a couple of low, rising buttes directly ahead of him and he made for them, looked in vain for a waterhole, finding nothing but a narrow crack in the middle of an area of sun-cracked soil where water had once bubbled from the ground and would probably do so again if the rains came. Dropping lightly from the saddle, he ground-hitched the horse, stretched his cramped, aching limbs, hitched the gunbelt up around his waist, then took out the jerked beef and bread from the saddlebag, cut off a couple of slices and sat down in the hot shade of the buttes to eat.

There was the deep stillness of the desert all about him and the clinging stillness made him relax a little in spite of the warnings that had been given him. Probably well-meant, he felt that they had, nevertheless, been greatly exaggerated.

Tilting the water bottle to his lips, he swilled the mouthful of water around his teeth for a few moments before allowing it to trickle down his throat. Setting the canteen down on the sand beside him, he stretched out on his back, reached up to draw his hat down over his eyes, then froze as a slug cracked into the rock behind him. The sound of the rifle shot was just reaching him when he made it to the edge of the butte, crouching down on his knees, watching the little puffs of dust that sprouted up from the ground as more bullets hounded him. The explosions of the shots echoed off the buttes, chasing each other off into the distance.

Legs braced, he slid down a steep slope, ending up in an arroyo carved deep at the bottom. A swift glance told him that the horse had stayed where it was, had not tugged the reins out of the ground and gone racing off. He breathed a silent prayer that he had trained that animal himself, had taught it all of the tricks the Apache taught their ponies.

When no more shots came from the hidden marksman, he reckoned he was in dead ground as far as the other was concerned. But there was a more than even chance that the bushwhacker had a spot picked out beyond revolver range and his Winchester was still in the scabbard beside the saddle. Lying flat on his stomach, he began to crawl towards the horse. A bullet broke the ground a little ahead of him and a second hummed through the air above his prone body as he got his legs under him and jumped for the horse, dropping down behind it, right hand reaching up for the stock of the rifle, dragging it clear of the scabbard.

The marksman in the distance pumped his shots regularly and accurately down as Everett turned and raced back for the arroyo. Then the firing ceased for a moment, but in those few seconds, he had caught a brief glimpse of the muzzle flashes of the rifle, knew where the other was hidden. Moving along the arroyo, he reached the far end, moving slow and careful, then stopped and risked a quick look around the edge. Nothing happened, so he reckoned that the dry-gulcher had not seen him, was probably watching the other end. The desert in front of him was absolutely quiet. Nothing moved. The other was lying low, waiting for him to show himself again. Or maybe he had a buddy somewhere around, who was trying to sneak up on him at that precise moment, to put a shot into his back.

Seconds dragged by. A herd of tiny flies buzzed around Everett's face and he dared not try to brush them away for fear of revealing his hiding place. When nothing happened after ten minutes, he slithered head first down the gullies, legs straight behind him so as not to raise any dust. There was a tall cluster of slab-sided rocks some two hundred yards away and one of them in particular, standing up a good head and shoulders above the rest seemed the logical hiding place for anyone intent on killing him. Sweat was running in little rivulets down his face and his shirt was sticking irritatingly to his back and shoulders as he wriggled forward, a few feet at a time.

He was more than a hundred yards from the rocks when he caught the sudden flicker of movement behind them. Swiftly, he jerked up his head, bringing up the Winchester at the same time, sighting it on a deep vee notch in the rocks. The man's head moved swiftly across his line of vision, was visible for less than a tenth of a second before it had vanished once more.

Rolling on to one side, he sent a couple of shots angling into the rocks, heard them shriek off the outcrops in high-pitched ricochet. Then the other had reached the end of the rocky tongue that thrust its way out into the desert. The next minute he had leapt across a short stretch of open space, down out of sight. Picking himself up, Everett raced forward, cocking the rifle as he did so. The start of a horse breaking into a run reached his ears as he gained the nearest rocks. Running over the spiny crest of the rocks, he saw the solitary rider spurring into the distance, kicking his mount's flanks to urge the last ounce of speed from it. The horse was a coal black stallion and the man had a light-coloured shirt and dark sombrero on the back of his head, but his face was turned away as he leaned forward over the saddlehorn to present a more difficult target for any slug coming after him from behind.

Reluctantly, Everett lowered the Winchester, walked forward with more confidence into the rocky gullies that lay before him. There was no danger from the other, but he might find some clue to the man's identity here among the boulders. He searched around, but all he discovered were a few empty cartridge cases where they had been spewed among the rocks as the other had levered the rapid action rifle. Examining one of the shells, he turned it over in his fingers for a moment and then tossed it away. More men used that calibre of cartridge than any other. He would learn nothing from them.

Going back to his horse, he climbed stiffly into the saddle, brushed some of the dust from his clothing, then moved out, heading west, with the sun gradually moving around on his left, until it was glaring in his eyes. There was a long, low bench of rock in the distance and he reckoned he should reach it by late afternoon, and Yuma lay just beyond it; unless there was another four-flusher waiting to drill him somewhere along the trail.

Jeb Kirby had lost his hat somewhere during the ambush and now, with the cool night wind beginning to blow along the main street of Yuma, drifting in off the sluggishly-flowing river, he felt cold and shivery as he brought the battered Murphy wagon to a grinding halt in front of the Overland yards. Behind him, the remaining wagons creaked and rumbled along the street, bringing several of the citizens and the small boys out in wonder, flocking around the oxen as the weary beasts stood sweating in the traces.

Suddenly there was an excitement in the long street that could be felt; it had come with the noise of the approaching wagons and the fact that there were wounded men lying in them, that one at least had been burned by fire, by flames which had been hurriedly hammered out, leaving tattered strips of blackened canvas trailing in the white dust.

Mary Vender heard the noise while the wagon train was still at the far end of the street and came hurrying out of the small office with Carmody trailing behind her. Hastily, she thrust her way between small groups of boys who stood with their mouths hanging foolishly open as they stared at the great wagons. Jeb lowered himself stiffly to the ground, tossed the thick leather reins on to the backs of the trembling oxen, then moved to meet her, his face worried, concerned.

'Jeb! Are you all right?' she asked anxiously.

'Got a bullet burn along my arm, but that'll keep,' he answered gruffly. 'But Shorty here has been hurt bad. Better get him to the doctor. He's lost a mite of blood. Some of the others aren't in too good a shape either.'

Mary turned to Carmody. 'See to that will you?' she said quickly. There was a hard note to her voice and her face was agate-still as she struggled with her thoughts, her eyes fixed ahead, her lips compressed. She said after a moment's pause: 'This is more of Quentin's doing. I'm certain of it.'

Elston had heard. He answered softly: 'You're right, Miss Vender; but you won't find it easy to prove. Even if you do get any proof, you think that Sheriff Paine is goin' to take your word against Quentin's?'

She gave him a strange look. 'Then we must take action ourselves to protect the freight line. I'm not going to be run out of Yuma just because a man like Earl Quentin moves in and thinks he can take over everything. There has to be a showdown here and maybe the time for it is getting very close.'

'You're askin' me and the boys to go up against Quentin and his men?'

'Yes,' she said. 'If it comes to that, then it's what I want you to do.'

Elston shrugged after a moment. 'I know how you feel. This thing has hit you hard, it's hit all of us. But I hate to hear coldness like this in a woman.'

'Now you're just set to start talking again, Matt,' she said coldly. She watched him so steadily in the gloom that he grew uneasy. He held her glance with an effort, knowing that he had never seen her like this since that day when word had come into town that her father had been found dead along the desert trail halfway between Yuma and Los Lobos. He knew that he had to show no weakness now, especially in front of her, but the effort cost him a lot and he eventually broke it by bringing a faint smile to his face.

'There's just the chance that you're jumpin' to the wrong conclusions here, Miss Vender,' he said. 'Could be that this outfit that hit the train was no part of his organisation at all. Those hills out yonder are full of men with the habits of wolves, who'll stop at nothin' to get their hands on gold. They could have figured that the boys were bringin' payment back with 'em on the return trip and–'

'You don't even believe that yourself, Matt,' she told him sharply. Her eyelids crept closer together as she spoke, accenting the hard look on her grim features. 'Come up into the office. I want to talk to you.'

Turning, she led the way, as the wagons were driven into the wide yards at the side of the office. She said nothing until they were in the small room, with the oil lamp burning on the table, throwing long, guttering shadows into the corners of the room. Then she looked at him, her troubled mind still not seeming to relax.

'Earl Quentin is still out of town, but Lander rode in half an hour ago. There was a stranger on the trail here, heading in from Los Lobos. Lander tried to scare him off when he saw that this man had deliberately left the trail and was skirting around it. He figured that it might have been the Morenci Kid.'

Elston felt a momentary tightening of the muscles of his stomach. He forced calmness into his tone. 'Did he manage to scare him off? My guess is that if it was the Morenci Kid, he didn't.'

'You're right. He only managed to get away himself. Best not to say anything of this to the rest of the boys. If they knew, we'd probably find ourselves without any teamsters by this time tomorrow.'

'You want me to keep an eye open in town in case this *hombre* rides in tonight?'

She nodded. 'Do that. But no trouble – mind. Not until we find out if he is the Kid and why he's in town.'

'I'll do that,' he said brusquely. He shook his head. 'If the Morenci Kid does ride into town and joins up with Quentin's outfit, this town is goin' to have a hell of a time very soon.' He paused, then asked 'That all?'

'All for now,' she answered.

When he had gone, she stood quite still in the quietness of the office, listening to the faint creak of the wagons down in the yard outside. She felt strange and oddly lonely. It was the first time since she had got over her father's death that this had happened to her. Always, she had felt so self-confident and assured. Now, within the space of a day or so, she felt lost, unable to grapple with the complex thoughts that continually filled her mind. She was undoubtedly a hard woman, she thought to herself; but in this frontier country, where every man's hand seemed to be set against his neighbour, one had to be hard and ruthless to survive. The country had killed her father, but she was absolutely determined that it wouldn't do the same to her. Perhaps she was made of sterner stuff than he had been; or maybe it was the mere fact of his death which had changed her, tempered her.

Sheriff Luke Paine was short, stout, going to fat. He chewed on the end of his cigar, holding it in the corner of his mouth, figuring that it made him seem a little more manly. It had been a bad day. What with the heat and the flies, and now the Overland team coming late into town with every sign that it had been hit somewhere along the trail – and hit hard. Sooner or later, Mary Vender would arrive at his office to register a formal complaint and demand that he form a posse and take some action against the culprits.

Trouble was, there would be no proof of who had done this, and although he had his own ideas on the subject – and no doubt she had too – there was still no reason why he should stir himself and try to make an arrest. Earl Quentin was a big man in Yuma now, one of the most influential and pretty soon, he'd probably be the biggest and Luke Paine was not going to go up against him just because Mary Vender asked him to do so. A woman had no business trying to run a freighting line anyway, he told himself. His cigar had gone out and he struck a sulphur match with an impatient gesture, applied the flame to the end of the cigar, inhaling deeply. Things would have been far better if she had only sold out when her pa had been killed, gone back East while she had the chance.

Earl Quentin had been bringing in hired killers for a little while now, he mused, feet up on top of the battered mahogany desk; and it was clear enough from this that he meant business. He'd be keeping most of these men under cover, so there was no way of connecting them with him and if it had been a party of his men that had jumped the

Overland wagons, Mary Vender would be able to prove nothing, even if those men of hers had brought in any dead men to back up their word.

There was a sharp knock on the door. Before he could swing his legs to the floor, the street door opened and the object of his thoughts came in. Hastily, he rose to his feet.

'Why, Miss Mary, it's a little late for a call like this, so I guess you're not here socially.'

'You guess right, Sheriff,' she said coldly. She declined his offer of a chair, stood in front of the desk, the lamplight playing over her features. Standing straight, he reckoned that she would perhaps be just a mite taller than him. Now however, she seemed a little smaller. Her figure was slight, almost boyish, but there were delicate feminine lines to her face in spite of the hardness that was now visible in it.

Sighing a little, he sat down in his chair, hands resting flat on top of the desk. 'I can guess why you're here, Mary,' he said gently. 'I saw the wagons roll into town a little while ago. What happened? An ambush?'

'That's right. Seems they were determined to wipe out the entire train and kill all of my men.' Her face was flushed now, looking down at him. 'I'm here to see what you intend to do about it?'

Paine spread his hands. 'What can I do, Mary? I can get a posse together, sure, and ride out there, look for clues. But you know as well as I do, that I'll find nothing.'

'*You* know as well as I do that this is Earl Quentin's work. He's smashed all of the smaller freighting companies and now that the Overland is the only one still opposing him in Yuma, he's doing things this way, just to be sure that he has the whole territory to himself.'

'Quentin has been out of town for almost a week now, Mary,' explained the other patiently. 'He isn't due back for a couple of days or so.'

'Sheriff, you know that Quentin could have left his orders before he took the stage out of town. Maybe he wanted to give himself an alibi. But it doesn't alter the facts. These were his men who attacked my wagons and—'

'Can you prove any of this, Mary?'

She shook her head bitterly. 'Like you said, Sheriff. Those killers will have left no clues. They'll have pulled out and taken their wounded and dead with them.'

'Then you know I can do nothin'. I can't

act on mere suspicion. I've got to have proof before I can make any arrests.'

'Don't you mean that you won't do anything because you daren't go against Quentin?'

'Now see here, Mary.' Paine thrust himself quickly to his feet, leaning forward over the desk. 'You go on talkin' like that and I'll have to warn you that you're triflin' with the law around here.' There was a bite of anger in his tone.

'If you don't understand then there's no use trying to talk and explain it to you.' Mary Vender moved back towards the street door. 'My father was murdered by Earl Quentin when he refused to sell out the Overland to him, but I didn't see you, or the law you're supposed to represent, doing anything about bringing his murderer to justice. Now this trouble has started and still you don't intend to do anything about it.' Pausing with her hand on the door handle, she said incisively, 'I suppose you haven't heard also that Quentin has sent word for the Morenci Kid to come into town and help him with his dirty work?'

'The Morenci Kid won't have any part of Quentin or Yuma,' said Paine thinly.

'You know this killer?'

65

'I've heard of him. You want my opinion? He just don't exist anywhere, except in the imagination of some folk who want to make a name for themselves. Some say he's an outlaw, a killer. Others reckon he's a bounty hunter.' His lips twitched into a faint grin. 'Some folk even say that he's a Federal Marshal working a lone walk pitch. He's a myth, like so many of these fast gunslingers.'

Mary hesitated. 'Then it may interest you to know that there's a stranger heading here from Los Lobos. From the way he acts, I'd say he's the Morenci Kid, whether you believe in him or not.' Turning, she opened the door, paused in the opening. 'Just one thing more, Sheriff. If the law won't give me protection for my wagon trains and Quentin is bringing in these hired gunhawks, then I intend to protect my interests in any way I see fit. When Quentin does get back, I suggest you tell him that two can play at his dirty game.'

'Now don't start anythin' you can't finish,' Paine began, then closed his mouth with a snap as he realised that he was talking to himself, that the street door had been closed and Mary Vender had gone.

After leaving his mount in the livery stable

halfway along the street, Everett walked through the lobby of the small hotel he had found at the corner of a small square within hailing distance of the river, woke a man he discovered lying sprawled in a wicker chair. The other grunted hoarsely, opened his red-rimmed eyes briefly, closed them for a moment, then stared up at the tall man who stood over him and decided that it might be better if he stayed awake. His gaze dropped for a moment to the Colt in the gunbelt slung low over the stranger's hips, then returned to the level eyes that gazed directly into his.

'What can I do for you, mister?'

'Guess you can give me a room for the night – arrange a bath, too, if that's possible. I'd sure like to get rid of this trail dust.'

'I can give you a room all right,' muttered the other, getting to his feet and moving around the corner of the desk. 'As for the bath, it'll take half an hour to heat the water, if that's all right.'

'Sure. Give me a call when it's ready.' Everett took the key the other handed him, made his way up the creaking stairs to the upper landing, along to the very end. All of the doors on either side were closed, he noticed and a thin slice of yellow light showed beneath two of them. The others were in darkness.

Opening his door, he glanced about him for a moment, dumped his saddle roll on the bed and, without lighting the lamp, walked over to the window and looked out. There was a low balcony that ran along the whole length of the building, making it possible for anyone to move from one room to the other. The catch on the window did not lock and after examining it for a moment, he turned away, shrugging his shoulders. Going over to the small table, he picked up the pitcher and drank half of the cold water it contained. He felt dry and brittle inside, just like a pine board that had been left lying too long in the sun, so that all of the moisture seemed to have been sucked from it.

The knock on the door came twenty minutes later. Locking the door after him, he followed the swamper down the stairs to a small curtained room at the back where a tin bath, half-full of steaming water stood in the middle of the stone floor. Stripping off his dust-covered clothes, he stepped into it and lay back, letting the warmth soak into his body, loosening the taut muscles, giving him a feeling of well being. He soaped himself all over, washing off the mask of dust and sweat which had caked over his features. His skin was tender beneath the dirt, had been scorched by the hot sun so that it stung painfully as the soap and water touched it.

When he was dressed again, he went along to the lobby, found the clerk still there, reading a newspaper.

'Any place in town where I could get a drink?' he asked.

Lowering the paper, the other said deferentially: 'There's a saloon just along the street, Mister Everett.'

'Thanks.' Everett half-turned, then glanced back at the other. 'You know a man in town called Quentin?' he asked.

The clerk's eyes opened wide for a fraction of a second. 'Earl Quentin. Why sure. He runs the Connaught Freighting organisation. One of the biggest in Yuma. Soon might be not only the biggest but the only freighting line running from here. You won't find him in town tonight though. He took the stage out about a week ago, headed East. Should be back in Yuma in two or three days though, if you'd care to hang around. Or maybe you could have a talk with his wagonmaster, fellow called Bat Elmore. More'n likely, you'll find him in the saloon this time of night.'

Everett considered that, didn't say anything for a long moment, then let his breath go in little pinches through his nostrils. 'You say the Connaught will be the only freight line operatin' from here?'

'That's the way things are shapin',' nodded the clerk. His face was flushed a little with importance as he imparted the news. 'Most of the smaller ones have folded up and been bought out by Quentin. Only the Overland still runnin' and judgin' from what happened this afternoon, that ain't likely to keep goin' much longer.'

Everett raised his brows a little. 'What did happen?'

'Ran into an ambush so they reckon. I saw the wagon train come in, just after sundown. Hard to say how many wagons they'd lost, maybe three, maybe six or more. They'd also lost some men, too. Mary Vender can't keep runnin' the line like this. Won't be long before half of her men fade over the hill, or go over to the Connaught line when Quentin starts offerin' higher wages and better conditions.'

Everett smiled grimly. 'I get the picture,' he said thinly. Nodding his thanks for the information, he made his way outside. Pausing on the boardwalk, he leaned his shoulders against one of the uprights, taking out the makings of a cigarette. As he rolled the quirly, he took stock of the street in front of him. A few yellow lights showed in square windows up and down the street and there came the thin, tinny notes of a piano from the saloon fifty yards away to his left. Light spilled out over the top of the batwing doors, slashing a swathe of radiance through the darkness. A handful of raucous voices were bellowing a song at the top of their lungs. Striking a match, he lit the cigarette, drew smoke into his lungs, then strode across the street to the saloon, pushing open the doors with the flat of his hands.

Going over to the bar, he lifted a finger, placed the weight of his shoulders on his elbows and waited for the bartender to bring the whisky over to him. Quite suddenly, he felt fine again. Excitement was a little electric current running through his body and he glanced into the broad mirror at the back of the counter, with the various bottles lined up on narrow shelves beneath it.

The barkeep seemed a trifle slow in bringing him the bottle and when he did arrive, he handed it across to him with a strained expression on his face. He stood there while Everett poured his drink, made no attempt to remove the bottle, just waited, his eyes fixed on the counter immediately in front of the other.

Lifting his head, Everett gave him a head-on glance. 'Somethin' on your mind, friend?' he asked gently.

Hastily, the other backed away, shaking his head swiftly. 'No, I guess not. Just that we don't see many strangers in Yuma. You just ridden in?'

'That's right. Left Los Lobos this mornin'.'

'Here on business, or just ridin' through?' The question came naturally from the other, but even as he spoke, Everett felt the tension in the saloon begin to rise, knew that every head was turned in his direction, waiting for his reply. There was something here he did not quite understand, some undercurrent at work in this town. Maybe, he thought tightly to himself, he had ridden into the middle of something big. Something to do with the freight lines, perhaps?

'I figure that's my business,' Everett said tautly. He drank down the whisky in a single gulp, then filled his glass a second time.

'Sorry, didn't mean to pry,' said the other,

stepping along the counter. He took out a wet cloth from his belt and began wiping up the stains on the bar.

Everett watched him for a moment, then turned back to his drink. He had not heard the man who came up beside him a few seconds later. Without turning his head, he glanced into the mirror behind the bar. The man was tall, a spare two inches or so shorter than Everett, but broader in the shoulders. There was a faint scar just visible near the hairline below his hat. Some time in the past, a slug had burned along the flesh at that point, leaving its mark for ever.

'Now suppose you tell me just why you are here, mister,' he said in a harsh, grating tone. 'Could be you're strange, and maybe you're not.' His glance, laid on Everett was one that believed nothing. 'You look like a man who's handy with a gun judgin' by your hardware.'

'I can usually get myself out of trouble if the need arises.'

'So I guessed. Trouble is, hell is about to bust wide open in Yuma and anybody who finds himself in the middle of it is likely to get himself shot at without any warnin'.'

'That meant as a threat or a warnin'?'

The other shrugged. 'Could be either. It's

up to you what you make of it. I work for Earl Quentin. He runs the Connaught organisation here in Yuma.'

'So?'

'So if you ever figure you've got a sixgun for sale, and you can prove you know how to use it, then I reckon we might be able to make use of a man like you. We've got several good men in the organisation already and one of the top-notch men comin' in on the stage any day now. There's the Overland Freight Line still holdin' out, but they won't be able to do that for long now. Some of the boys hit 'em good and hard this afternoon. Might take a few more incidents like that to fix 'em for good and all, but it won't be long now.'

'Maybe the Overland are fixin' to fight back?' Everett answered calmly.

The other's eyes narrowed to a slit, the black brows drew together into a single straight line. There was an instant hardening on the other's face, then he shook his head slowly, meaningly.

'Not a chance. And when the Morenci Kid gets here, it'll be the finish.'

Everett let his expression slip for a moment. 'You bringin' in that killer to run these folk out of Yuma?' he said sharply. The other grinned viciously. 'Can't think of any better way of doin' it – and fast. Now, are you interested in the job or not. Stick around Yuma and you'll have to come in on one side or the other; and don't let sentiment sway you when you find that the Overland is bein' run by a woman.'

'I never let sentiment interfere with any business,' Everett said tightly. 'Nor do I agree with bringin' in gunslingers like the Morenci Kid.'

'You know this *hombre*?' queried the other.

'Heard of him,' Everett corrected. 'They say he's a cold-blooded killer. If this *hombre* Quentin is hirin' him, then it can only be for one reason.'

The other's eyes glinted. 'Sure, and why not? There's a fortune to be picked up here, runnin' the Army supplies from Yuma to all points north and west. But there can be only one freight line runnin' in the territory. There's no place for two and Mister Quentin has got this place dead to rights.'

'So it seems.' Everett dropped the butt of his cigarette on to the floor and ground it out with his heel.

'You interested in that job? I got the authority to hire you if you are, on Mister Quentin's say-so.'

'I'll think about it,' Everett said softly. He found himself disliking this bragging bully of a man; had already guessed at his true nature from the first moment he had met him.

A mean look crept into the other's eyes. He said shortly: 'Better make up your mind fast, mister. Maybe the offer won't be open this time tomorrow.'

Everett grinned slightly. 'If that's so, I might just get myself a job with the Overland Company.'

The wagonmaster eyed him up and down for a moment, an expression on his face as if he had not been able to believe his ears.

After a few moments, he said ominously: 'That would be a real big mistake, stranger. Real big. A man could get himself shot up actin' like that here in Yuma with things as they stand right now.'

'I get the message,' Everett said harshly. He downed his drink, turned his back on the other and walked slowly out of the saloon.

3

THE TURNING SCREW

The stage from Tucson and Los Lobos came boiling along the main street of Yuma and stopped in front of the Clinton Hotel. Two men climbed down from the coach and walked into the hotel. While the man carrying the Winchester clambered down the other side, swinging himself easily into the street, the third passenger alighted, took the grip which the driver handed down to him, glanced up and down the street for the moment, then clamped his thick lips more tightly around the expensive cigar, blew a cloud of smoke into the air and followed the other two into the hotel, going immediately to the room at the end of the second floor, a corner room which looked down on to the street.

Earl Quentin had been there for less than ten minutes when there came a knock at the door and three men entered. Lounging at his ease on the bed in front of the window,

Quentin shifted his bulk on the pillows which he had bolstered up behind him, legs stretched out straight in front of him.

'Sit down, gentlemen,' he said, motioning towards the chairs. He settled his shoulders more deeply into the pillows. George Frew, the banker, a fussy little man in a black frock coat and white side-whiskers, lowered himself carefully into the wicker chair a few feet away, sitting on the very edge of it, as if expecting to have to rise to his feet in a hurry at any moment. Cranston, long and thin, drooped in his chair, hunched back, eyes fixed on Quentin. His dark eyes only seldom showed any hint of the way his mind worked, although occasionally they would gleam with an inner excitement, showing as a reflected shine in the deep depths. That glint was there now as he took out a flat tin and extracted a cigarette from it, placing it carefully between his pinched lips, lighting it and blowing the smoke in front of him in a sharp exhalation.

'I reckon it would have been hard to time things better than we did, Earl,' he said, grinning a little. 'The Overland lost four of their wagons out on the trail, half a day's ride from Yuma, just as we planned.'

Over by the window, Bat Elmore peered

down into the sun-hazed street. It was almost as if he was making sure that what they said in this room could not be over-heard by anyone down there.

Quentin watched him curiously for a moment with a flat stare. He felt inwardly satisfied. That was the action of a really cautious man. Men such as Frew and Cranston did not pause to think of these things. They were shallow men, content to allow things to go on from day to day, never really planning ahead. But Elmore was careful, which was possibly the reason why he had stayed alive for so long.

Quentin said to him: 'You sure that you have everything taken care of, Bat? No loose ends hangin' out that anybody can take hold of and pull out to see what lies at the other end?'

Elmore nodded sombrely. 'All seen to, boss,' he said harshly. 'It was real easy. We lost six men, but we can get more whenever we want 'em. This territory is runnin' with gunslingers who're runnin' away from the law.'

Quentin nodded as though satisfied with the answer. Opening his mouth, he let out a cloud of smoke. Waving the cigar, he glanced at Frew. 'This is where you earn your money,

George. Mary Vender will soon need a loan to cover the losses on her wagon team. We know she's bein' forced to cut her freightin' rates down to the bone. You know what you have to do when she comes to the bank for an extension?'

Frew nodded. 'It won't be easy. She's a pretty determined woman, but I'll refuse any application for a loan.'

'Just as you did the other lines when they came, eh?' grinned Elmore from the window. 'Must say she's held out longer than we figured.'

'She's virtually finished now,' Quentin laughed, waving his cigar in little circles. 'She'll be only too glad to see things our way and come to terms with us. Our terms!' he added softly.

Frew nodded. 'Sure, Earl, sure. Our price, if that's the way you want it.' He sounded just a little dubious and Quentin was quick to notice it.

'You got somethin' on your mind, George? You don't sound too happy about the deal.'

'Only one thing worryin' me, Earl. You know that the Overland has been freighting supplies for the Army for more'n fifteen years now, ever since they set up their posts along the border. They may start askin' awkward questions when we try to go through with this and put in our bid.'

'Let 'em. We've got nothin' to worry about. They can't pin anythin' on us. The Army is tied to the purse-strings of the politicians in Washington and if we make an offer that undercuts anyone else, they'll jump at it and ask no questions. The bigger the organisation, the lower our runnin' costs.'

Frew raised his brows at that, stared at the tip of his cigarette. 'But when you gain control of this territory, what then? Start puttin' up the freight rates for the Army and they'll maybe begin diggin' into things that are best left buried.'

Quentin's face was bland. 'So they may start diggin'. But it'll be too late then for anybody to do anythin' about it and they'll have no proof that we were behind these unfortunate incidents that have befallen the Overland organisation.' His smile broadened. He sat up a little, a man seemingly content with life. 'And besides, if we can squeeze the homesteaders, we may not need to raise the freightin' rates for the Army. Now put that thought out of your mind, George. Just leave all of the worryin' to me. All you have to do is see that Mary Vender

81

doesn't get another loan. After that, I'll give her a month, maybe not as long as that before she comes crawlin' to me, beggin' me to take the Overland off her hands.'

'She's got some tough men in her teams,' Elmore said soberly. 'What if they decide to fight?' He took a couple of turns up and down the room, eyes shadowed darkly in speculative thought.

'You forgettin' the Morenci Kid?' Quentin had listened carefully to the other, his eyes pinched deeply, hiding everything that went on in his mind. 'I sent that wire for him a few days ago. He ought to be in town soon.'

'You sure he'll come?'

'He'll be here. I made him an offer he just can't refuse. A high sum, but it will be worth it to me in the end.' He stubbed out his cigar, rubbed the tips of his blunt fingers together. 'I've been waiting for this for a long time. You all know that, just bidin' my time for the right conditions to come along. When things began shapin' up my way, I knew nothin' could stop me. First that unfortunate accident to Clem Vender. Then the chance to squeeze all of the other freighting lines out of business, George here calling in the loans when they came due, and now the Morenci Kid headin' this way to finish everythin' off for me.' He sighed melodramatically. 'Pity that Mary Vender decided to hold out like she did. Surprised me the way she held on. I'd figured her for one of these women who'd cut and run back East when things got tough. Reckon we all have to underestimate somebody once in our lives.'

He paused for comment and receiving none, went on: 'You're all sure that nothin' has happened while I've been away that I ought to know about?' He looked penetratingly at the three men facing him, eyeing each in turn.

When neither of the other two men said anything, Bat Elmore spoke up. 'A stranger rode into town last night, put up at the hotel down the street. I braced him in the saloon, tried to find out somethin' about him. He seemed a reticent sort of *hombre* to me, maybe a man with somethin' in his past he wants to hide.'

'You get anythin' out of him at all?'

'Only that he'd ridden in from Los Lobos. I figured him for a drifter, even offered him a job, but he said he'd just think it over. Must say he looked a mite scared when I mentioned the Morenci Kid.'

Quentin lit another cigar, inhaled deeply,

reflectively. 'I don't like men movin' around town that I know nothin' about. Inclined to make me feel nervous. We'd better find out who he is and what he wants. Get over to the hotel, see what you can come up with on him. He might be a Federal Marshal pussy-footin' it around.'

'Why should they be interested in Yuma?'

'Don't talk like a fool, Bat!' snapped the other, showing his first signs of anger. 'Those men we ran out of town when we took over their freight lines. Some of 'em may have talked back East. If they did, a marshal might have been sent to look things over.'

'All right,' said Elmore. 'I'll be along there pronto. You want me to have some of the boys take care of him if—'

'No!' Quentin jerked the word out. 'We've got to play this easy. Find out who he is and what he's doin' here. We'll decide then what to do about him. I want to know this before the Morenci Kid gets here.' He chewed on his cigar for a moment, frowning. 'This could mean trouble. I don't like it. If there is a Federal Marshal runnin' around on the loose somewhere out there it could mean we'll have to alter some of our plans. Now get along, Bat.'

He waited until the other had slipped out of the room, closing the door softly behind him, then eased himself off the bed and walked over to the window, narrowing his eyes to slits as he stared down into the harsh sunglare that bounced off the dusty street below, the heat rising from it in shimmering waves.

'You hold any overdue paper on the Overland Company, George?' he asked presently, without turning his head.

Frew shifted a little in his chair. 'No. So far they've always managed to stay clear of an overdraft.'

'But if we were to put in a low offer for the Army stores that are due in on the paddle steamer the day after tomorrow and Mary Vender loses that particular contract, what then?'

'Then it's my guess she'll find things hard. It's one of the biggest contracts there is, comes in regularly every other month. It's a long haul out to those outposts the Army run near the California border, through some of the worst territory hereabouts and that's sayin' plenty.'

'You reckon she might have a chance of shippin' those stores out with the men and wagons she's still got left, Cranston?'

'Could be. She'll go for that contract before any of the others. Her pa built up the company on the Army business and she ain't likely to let it drop without a struggle.'

Quentin nodded. 'Then I guess I'd better take myself along and have a word with the colonel. A word in his ear could put us in the runnin' for that contract.'

Wayne had risen late and breakfasted late. It was a fine, clear morning when he stepped out into the street and made his way down to the waterfront. The bright glare of sunlight on the smooth river presaged another hot day. There were several small boats around, some tied up at the quay, others either moving in or slipping their moorings and churning their way down the river and out of sight around the bend in the distance. Men worked in the hot sun on the quayside, toting huge barrels and bales of cotton. Here and there, he saw a few blue uniforms, remembered that there was a large Army headquarters here in Yuma and recalled what he had heard of the outposts that were scattered throughout the desert and mountain country to the north and west of the town.

He leaned his chest on a tall post that rose out of the stonework of the quay and surveyed the scene through narrowed eyes. His breakfast had wrought a feeling of well-being in him and he was content to stand there and let the sun soak into him. He had slept well during the night, the first time he had slept in a comfortable bed for more than a week and already he was feeling the benefit of it.

He had been there for almost five minutes when he heard the soft step at his back and was accosted by a tall, sombre-faced individual who wore a jaunty air and a star on his shirt that glinted in the sun whenever he moved.

'Your name Everett?' inquired the other harshly. He let his gaze wander up and down the tall man.

'That's right.' Everett pushed himself easily away from the post and stood up. 'Somethin' wrong, Sheriff?'

'That's as may be.' The other's face showed no sign of friendliness. Rather there was suspicion written all over his pinched features, visible in the narrowed eyes. 'You rode into town last night and put up at the hotel yonder.'

'Now why should that bother you? Am I supposed to have done somethin' against the law?'

'Maybe there's plenty you've done that we don't know about here in Yuma.' The other's brow was furrowed and Everett guessed that his mind was flicking over the pages of a wanted book, trying to figure out if his face was known to him. 'We've got a lawful society here and I aim to keep it that way, which means that I like to know everythin' about any strangers who might ride in unannounced, specially if they come totin' hardware that shows plenty of signs of havin' been used in the past.' He rubbed his chin. 'I don't want to inconvenience you, mister, but I'd appreciate it if you'd step along to the office for a talk.'

Everett comprehended. In spite of the other's assertions about law and order in Yuma, there were sure to be some characters around who would be mighty interested in knowing who he was and what he might be doing there; men who had their own axe to grind, and wanted no one butting in on their plans. He said thinly: 'I've got plenty of time, Sheriff. But this is too good a day to waste sittin' inside some gloomy office. Can't we discuss things out here?'

Paine's cold eyes regarded the other steadily for a moment, then he shrugged his shoulders, nodded. 'Fair enough, Everett.

Where do you come from?'

'Tucson. All points north and east. You mention it and I'll have been there sometime.'

'That answer just turns back on itself and means nothin',' snorted the other. 'I reckon you'll have to do better than that to satisfy me.'

Everett said carelessly, 'Seems to me I don't have to satisfy anyone, Sheriff, unless you've got somethin' you want to try to pin on me.' He stared at the lawman curiously. 'My opinion is that somebody in town is mighty anxious to find out things about me and they've made it their business to put this into your mind and get you to do it for 'em. Somebody like Quentin or that wagonmaster of his, Elmore.'

Paine shook his head. Evidently, thought Everett, he did not intend to let himself be drawn so easily. 'I'm askin' these questions for my own peace of mind, mister,' he said tartly. 'I don't aim to have any *hombres* who figure themselves to be quick at flashin' a gun, moving in and tryin' to start trouble here.' He added with a faint hint of irony, 'I'm tellin' you this so you won't get any funny ideas about lettin' things get out of hand.'

'You sound as if there's trouble a-brewin' here already, Sheriff,' he said innocently. 'I heard a little of it last night in the saloon. Fella by the name of Quentin, moving in and trying to grab off all of the freightin' business for himself and not carin' much how he does it.'

Paine's mouth hardened, compressed into a thin line. 'Talk like that is goin' to land you in big trouble around here. If things are left as they are, it's more'n likely that the boss of the Overland Company will see sense and things can be settled amicably.'

'Mary Vender, you mean?'

For a second, a look of surprise flitted over the sheriff's face, but it was gone almost at once. 'That's right,' he muttered. 'You know her?'

'Nope. But I always was one for seeing that folk got a fair crack of the whip, no matter whether it's a man or a woman.' He smiled cheerfully. 'I reckon I might even step over there and offer her my services.'

'If you do that, then you're a fool.' Anger touched the other's tone, lifting it in pitch a little. 'My advice is, don't push your luck and poke your nose into business that don't concern you.'

Everett's smile did not change, but there

was something subtly different in his bearing that was not unnoticed by the sheriff. 'Then I gather that you're backin' Quentin.'

'Maybe Quentin is the kind of man we need around here. A man strong enough to prevent the lawless elements from movin' in and takin' over.'

Everett pushed back his hat, wiping a rim of sweat away from his forehead with his finger. 'Seems to me that this should be your kind of job, Sheriff. And I fail to see how Quentin is goin' to keep the lawless breed in line by tryin' to run the Overland Freighting Company out of business and bringin' in gunslingers like the Morenci Kid from back east.'

'I've heard nothin' of any gunslingers movin' in,' declared Paine harshly.

'Then I figure you're way behind the times, Sheriff. Quentin knows he's due in because he's the one who hired him. By now, I reckon most of the town knows.' He prodded the other with a stiff forefinger, grinning a little viciously to emphasise his words. 'If you're lookin' for troublemakers in Yuma, better start checkin' on the men that Quentin is hirin'.'

'Could be I'll do that,' acknowledged the other. 'But just heed my warnin'. Don't get yourself into a tangle with anybody in Yuma. You could find yourself way out on a limb with someone sawin' you off from the tree.' Turning sharply on his heel he strode off along the quayside, spurs jingling a little.

Half an hour later, Everett was standing outside the door of the offices of the Overland Freighting Company at the top of the flight of wooden steps that led up from the big yard. As he stood there, he glanced over the Murphy wagons that stood in a long line against the wooden fencing at the far side. A couple of men in overalls were busy greasing the axles. They paid no attention to him and even the small group of men who came from a single-storied building and walked across the yard did not give him a second glance.

Rapping with his knuckles on the door, he waited a moment and then pushed it open. A short, sparse man was seated behind a desk at the far side of the room. He got hesitantly to his feet as Wayne went in, his eyes widening a little as he let his gaze wander from the other's face down to the gun slung low on Everett's hip.

'Can I do anythin' for you, mister?' asked Carmody sibilantly. He was not sure whether he liked the look of this man or not. His first impression was that here stood a gunman sent over by Quentin, but he hastily revised his opinion as Wayne said softly: 'I was told I could find Mary Vender here, boss of this outfit.'

'She's at the Army Headquarters right now,' Carmody said. 'I'm the clerk here. Maybe I can help you.'

'Depends. I figured she might give me a break. I'm after a job.'

'A job?' The other's brows lifted a little. He sat down behind the desk, scratched his ear. 'Guess you must be new in town.'

'You mean you don't have any jobs goin'?' Everett inquired innocently.

'Oh no. Just that things are pretty difficult right now. If you're lookin' for a job with pay and the prospects of livin', then you'll be wantin' the Connaught organisation down the street a piece.'

Wayne nodded. 'Noticed their place on the way here. Trouble is, I bumped into their wagonmaster and some of his boys last night in the saloon. Didn't take to 'em at all. Figured I might try here first.'

'Why don't you hire on with Earl Quentin?'

Wayne turned slowly and glanced appraisingly at Mary Vender as she entered the room. She did not look away from him, but held his glance as direct as his had been. Her eyes were cool, almost indifferent, and there was a look on her face, a challenging expression that seemed to dare him to break her air of reserve and composure.

'Like I was sayin', I figured I didn't like the men who work for Quentin. Besides, I don't like to see anyone trampled on by big men such as the Connaught boss.'

She gave him a deeply studying glance and for a moment there seemed to be some answer balanced in her mind; then she shrugged her shoulders a little and walked past him into the office.

'Can you handle that gun you're carrying?' she asked.

'If I have to.'

'If you intend working for me, you'll have to.' She took off the wide-brimmed hat, laid it on the desk, shaking her head so that the long hair moved softly on her shoulders. 'Quentin is trying to ruin me. He had a bunch of his men ambush the wagon train on its way back into Yuma, killed some of my men and burned four of the wagons. Now he's been to the colonel to try to get the contract to move the supplies that will be coming in on the steamer the day after to-morrow. I had to lower my price to keep that contract. We're working at the very bottom of the barrel now. I can't afford to pay the wages that Quentin can offer.' A pause, then: 'And if we don't carry out the conditions of the contract, the Overland is finished.'

'And Quentin knows this, I presume?'

'I'm sure he does.' She looked at him with a moment's penetrating attention. 'You still want to work for me?'

'Nothin' you've just told me makes me want to change my mind.'

'Then you can consider yourself hired. Matt Elston is my wagonmaster. He's a hard man but a fair one. You'll find him in the yard. Tell him I just hired you.'

Everett smiled a little, gave a brief nod, then went out, down the steps. He found a small group of men standing near one of the wagons, carrying out minor repairs. They looked up as he reached them.

'You know where I can find Elston?' he asked.

A grizzled oldster spat a stream of brown tobacco juice into the dirt, then jerked a thumb towards the low-roofed building to the rear. 'You'll find him in there,' he said hoarsely.

'Thanks.' He made his way over, had just reached the door when it was thrust open and a stocky, broad-shouldered man came out. He gave Everett a sharp look.

'You'll be Elston, the wagonmaster,' Everett said quietly.

The big man nodded. He said nothing, waiting for the other to go on.

'My name is Everett. I've just had a word with Miss Vender. She said to tell you she just hired me.'

The other stared at him in surprise for a moment, then uttered a harsh laugh. 'You came here and asked for a job with the Overland?' The situation seemed to tickle him more than ever. 'You're a salty young cuss. Damn me if you ain't. Reckon though that you don't know what you're lettin' yourself in for, joinin' up with us. Quentin has sworn to smash this outfit and by God, he really means to do it. Guess you just don't know how long your job here is likely to last.'

'So I've been told,' Everett said quietly. 'There seem to be plenty of folk, on both sides of the line, who have tried to talk me out of comin' here for a job. Fella by the name of Bat Elmore offered me a job last night in the saloon. He seemed mighty peeved when I turned it down.'

'Reckon he must have thought you was plain loco,' grunted the other. He nodded towards the wagons. 'We had twenty of those a few weeks ago. Then a lot of unexplained accidents have been happenin' until now we only have twelve. We lost four yesterday.'

'Reckon things might turn out to be excitin' after all,' said Everett innocently.

'Exciting! That what you figure it is to have your companions shot to pieces all around you? Too many guns seem to be pointed this way for my likin'.'

'There must be a better way of doin' this,' said George Frew hesitantly. He sat bolt upright in the wicker chair where he had been seated that morning, his fingers twisting and interlacing in front of him. Like his hands, his face was all twisted up into lines of worry and alarm.

'There's no better way, goddamn,' said Quentin harshly. He hammered a clenched fist into the palm of his hand. 'I made my try this morning, to get that Army contract. I cut my offer to what I figured would be below anythin' that Mary Vender could match. Yet in spite of that, Colonel Parker calmly informs me that the contract for those supplies has been awarded to the Overland Freighting Company as in the past.'

'Guess there's nothin' you can do about that,' muttered Cranston from the corner of the room.

'Isn't there, by God,' roared Quentin. His face was flushed, both from anger and the effect of the whisky he had drunk. 'We'll see about that. They'll start loadin' up the supplies as soon as the steamer docks. It'll take 'em the best part of a day to complete it, even if they start in the early mornin'. That means they'll move the wagons back to their yard and keep 'em there for the night, before movin' out the next day.'

'So?'

Quentin clamped his teeth tightly around the cigar. He puffed furiously on it for a long moment, then spoke around it. 'So we hit 'em durin' the night when the loaded wagons are ready and waitin'.'

'Hit 'em – how?' inquired Frew. A trembling hand ran up and down his cheek.

Quentin sat back, grinned suddenly, lips twisted away from his teeth like those of an animal scenting its prey. 'Seems to me from what the boys tell me, those fire arrows worked well the last time they were used. Guess we'd better use fire this time. Only now we'll make sure that the whole wagon train gets it. Pity about the Army stores, but that will be Mary Vender's worry, not ours.'

Elmore's chair creaked alarmingly as he stirred himself in it. For once, his sullen features were lit by a faint grin. 'I like that idea, boss,' he said harshly. 'I'll get a couple of the boys to go with me. You can rely on us to finish the job this time.'

'I still say it could be dangerous,' Frew persisted stubbornly. He looked from one man to the other, his adam's apple bobbing up and down nervously in his throat.

'You don't reckon that Paine is goin' to have any grouse, do you?' said Quentin.

'I wasn't thinking of Paine. He won't interfere. But what about this *hombre* who rode in yesterday – Everett? Anybody found out who he is? Could be a Federal Marshal and that's a horse of a different colour. We may have Sheriff Paine in our pocket, but you won't bribe a marshal.'

'If he makes any try to interfere, we'll drop him,' grated Quentin. 'But if you carry out orders, I don't see any reason why there should be any trouble. If they have anybody on guard, you know what to do.'

'Sure. You got no call to worry, boss.' Elmore gave a quick nod. 'Those wagons will go up like dry tinder.'

Quentin laughed harshly. 'That's it, Bat. Dry tinder. Pity the Army will have to go short of rations for the next two or three weeks until we can bring in our own teams.' He pursed his lips thoughtfully. 'And, of course, that could push up the price a lot higher than that I gave Colonel Parker today.'

4

THE DESTROYERS

It had been a quiet evening in the saloon. A few of the usual drifters had come and gone and now only a handful of them were left, playing faro at one of the tables in the corner. Wayne Everett, leaning on the counter had been merely killing time, talking with Flint Errol, the bartender, and watching the card game with little real interest. The hard day's work at the quayside in the blistering Arizona heat had raised a deep thirst in him and here, at least, the beer was plentiful and cool. He had seen nothing of the men of the Connaught organisation all afternoon although during the early part of the morning a few of them had drifted down to the quayside, lounging against the wooden pilings, watching with flat, expressionless eyes as the heavy barrels and crates were unloaded from the deck of the paddle-steamer and carried by sweating men to the waiting Murphy wagons where other men waited to heave them on board, stacking them in the back, tying them down securely with thick, hempen ropes.

Everett had half expected an attempt to be made to stop them. When nothing had happened and they had got the wagons safely into the yard and behind the locked gates for the night, his apprehension had increased rather than diminished. Judging by his character, Earl Quentin was not the sort of man to take the loss of the Army contract lying down. There was a plan being built up against them somewhere right now and he wished he knew what it was.

Perhaps another ambush on the trail once they were well clear of Yuma, thought the other, though somehow he didn't think so. Two attacks on the Overland wagons and the Connaught ones going through unmolested would be far too much of a coincidence and the long finger of accusation would be pointed directly at Quentin for everybody to see. Even the Army might start to take a hand in things since it would be their supplies that were destroyed.

No, if Quentin did intend to do something, it would be subtle and cunning, arranged so that nothing could be proved against him.

The doors of the saloon, creaking as they

swung, opened to let in the trio of men. Everett stiffened a little as he recognised Bat Elmore and two of his cronies. They barged up to the counter, set themselves against it, feet resting on the low rail, deliberately ignoring him. Not until Errol had passed along the bottle and three glasses did they say anything, then Bat turned to Everett, a darkly vicious grin on his swarthy features. From the flush on his face it was clear that he had been drinking already. He looked about as innocent as a rattler poised to strike.

'Hear you not only turned down that offer I made a couple of days ago, but you went over to the Overland Company.' His tone was deliberately provocative and insulting.

'Then I guess you heard right, Elmore.' Wayne turned a little away from the bar so that he was facing the other directly. 'Though I don't see what business it is of yours who I decide to work for.'

Elmore's grin thinned down a little. Glancing at the men behind him, he growled: 'Listen to him, boys. Rides into town from no place at all and he ain't here more than a couple of days before he gets it into his head that he's the cock o' the walk.'

The two men laughed harshly; one with a

high-pitched braying laugh like a jackal. 'Guess he'll soon have to learn to step easy around Yuma, Bat.'

'If he should live that long.' Elmore had turned back now, his eyes fixed on Everett's face.

'Now there ain't no call for startin' any trouble in here, Bat,' Errol spoke up placatingly from behind the bar as he sidled away from the trio.

Still without shifting his gaze, Elmore said: 'You just keep out of this little matter, Errol; and stay away from the bar. Make a move towards that shotgun you've got stacked away behind there and Torro here is likely to make sure it's the last move you ever make.'

Errol stopped, wet his lips nervously. Then he edged away to the back of the bar. Finishing his drink in a single gulp, setting the glass down on the counter, Elmore shifted his stance a little, moving out towards the centre of the room. Taking his Colt carefully from its holster, using his fingertips, he dropped it on to the bar.

'This is just between you and me, Everett,' he muttered thickly. 'I don't aim to kill you. I figure that if you're still around we can leave that to the Morenci Kid when he hits town. But right now you need a lesson and

I aim to give it you.

'You can talk pretty loud when you've got two *hombres* with guns to back your play.' Wayne nodded towards the two gunslingers lounging near the bar. The Mexican-looking one named Torro looked particularly dangerous.

'Put up your hardware next to mine, boys.' Bat Elmore waited until the clatter of the guns on the counter at his back signalled that this had been done. 'Now we shall see if you can back your mouth with deeds,' he gritted, stepping slowly towards Wayne.

Slowly, Wayne unbuckled the heavy gunbelt, laid it on the bar. There was something wrong here, he reflected. Elmore was a tall man for sure, almost as tall as he was, wiry but not too solid. He might be a real dirty fighter, but he did not look the sort who would want to mix it with anyone unless he had the edge on his side. Not until he had stepped away from the bar did he hear the warning cry from Errol and the harsh chuckle from one of the watching men. Bat's right hand had moved, but not forward. It snaked behind his back, came into view a moment later holding the long, coiled rawhide whip carried by most of the teamsters.

Flicking it viciously, the other sent it hissing across the few feet that separated them. Instinctively, Wayne stepped back, felt the bar jam hard across his shoulders. The tip of the whip slashed his sleeve and he felt the red-hot sting on his flesh. Glancing down, he saw the streak of blood on his arm through the long tear in the cloth. Another shearing slash across his cheek this time and he heard Elmore's harsh bellow of laughter.

For a second, the pain seared agonisingly through his brain. Then rage, cold and malignant flared up inside him, burning every other emotion away. Perhaps it was this which saved him from the worst beating of his life. Any other man, faced with a similar situation, might have cringed there against the bar, forced to take what was coming to him.

But there leapt within Everett that sense of savage anger that overrode all else, un-reasonable, unaccountable. His subsequent actions were neither reasoned out nor planned in any way. He paid no heed to Errol's shout, nor to his own pain as the whip crashed across his shoulders for the third time. He did not even see Elmore clearly, only as a vague and blurred shadow wavering through the red haze. Swiftly, he launched himself forward, kicking off from the bar with his heels. His lowered head hit Elmore full in the stomach, the impact driving the other back against one of the tables. It splintered beneath their combined weight and they went down with Elmore struggling desperately to use the whip. But at such close quarters it was more of a hindrance than a weapon. As the table smashed under them, they rolled apart. Shaken and jolted, each man climbed slowly to his feet, facing one another. Elmore's features were twisted into a grimace of agony and his throat muscles worked as he strove to draw air down into his lungs. Eyes narrowed, still gripping the whip, he tried to lift it again, to bring it slashing down, but Wayne was too fast for him. He went in low and swift, took the down chopping blow of the whip handle on his shoulders, then rammed in two hard punches to the other's chest and stomach, driving him back. As the other wilted, Everett straightened, sent his fist smashing into the other's face. There was the solid, satisfying feel of cartilage bursting under his knuckles and instantly a crimson stain dripped down the Connaught man's chin from his mashed nose.

The punch shook up the other. Even as he

tried to regain his balance and move forward, Wayne struck down at his wrist and the rawhide whip dropped from nerveless fingers on to the floor. Without pausing to look down, Wayne kicked it under the tables, sending it skidding into the far corner of the saloon.

'Now we'll do this on even terms,' Wayne grunted. The cold anger still burned in him, but he knew that he would need more than this to beat the man who faced him. There was a rough, toughness in the other which he had not allowed for at first. Elmore had been brought up in a hard school, knew every dirty trick of in-fighting, was not reluctant to use any of them.

A rifling right fist caught the Connaught wagonmaster under the left eye, sent him staggering back with a wild yell. His spurs caught in the leg of one of the chairs, pitching him down on to his back. Everett did not wait for him to get up, but threw himself down on top of the man, fingers reaching savagely for his exposed throat, squeezing powerfully. Elmore's eyes bulged, threatened to pop out of their sockets and a painful gurgling came from the depths of his throat.

Then came a surging reaction from the

other. Half-stunned, the big man's arms lifted, grabbing at Everett's wrists while at the same time, he kicked up with his legs, heaving himself over on to his side, throwing the other off. Lurching to his feet, drawing in air in great rasping breaths, he stood bent slightly forward from the hips, arms hanging by his side, long fingers curled into taloned claws. His lips were puffed and blood continued to drip from his chin from his smashed nose and mouth. But there was still plenty of fight left in him. His hair, drooping over his eyes gave him a wild and ferocious look. A low growl rumbled from his throat as he moved in to the attack, arms swinging in wide arcs.

Wayne waited patiently, then stepped nimbly to one side, feinting with his right and setting the other up for a quick and powerful jab to the face. The blow merely seemed to infuriate the other more. Gathering himself, he bored in, his head lowered, arms closing as he caught Everett around the waist in a bear-hug, striving to bend him back so that he could use his weight to snap the other's spine. Now, there seemed no intention in the other's mind just to beat Wayne up a little and leave it to the Morenci Kid to finish him, as he had threatened earlier. The blow to his pride and the pain in his body when it had seemed he was on the point of losing this fight, had burned all of that away. Now his eyes were filled with the killer lust. Wayne knew that nothing would satisfy the other now than his own death. This was to be a fight to the finish as far as Elmore was concerned.

Savagely, Elmore tightened his grip, his fingers interlaced in the small of Wayne's back. His face was thrust deeply into Wayne's shoulder, lowered so that he could not reach it. His breathing came harsh and rasping as he increased the pressure. Bracing his legs, Wayne knew that he would soon have to break this hold or perish. He could not hold out much longer. The human spine had only a limited ability to resist such pressure and then it was forced to snap.

Pain lanced through his body as he was forced back by the other's weight leaning on him. It was becoming more and more difficult for him to breathe and there was a sharp agonising pain in his chest each time he forced down a ragged gust of air. Then he was rammed hard against the bar and out of the corner of his eye he could see Elmore's two sidekicks grinning viciously to themselves as they watched.

With an effort, he managed to lean away from the bar a little way, then slammed back. The move caught Elmore's hands hard against the unyielding wood and he grunted with pain. Ignoring the pounding in his head, Wayne repeated the performance. There was a small projection on top of the counter and at the same time that his hands were being smashed against the bar, his arms were being bent against this projection, and with a sudden yell of pain, Elmore released his hold. For a moment, everything was blurred. He could just make out Elmore as a wavering shadow hovering at the limit of his vision. He knew he had to finish this before Bat had another chance to move in, but it was difficult to get his whirling mind into focus again. By the time he succeeded, the other was moving forward once more, shaking his head slowly from side to side, brushing the strands of lank hair out of his eyes with the back of his left hand. Everett let him come, noticed the other's knee poised to smash him in the groin and swung his body out of the way as it came thrusting forward. He felt it graze his side, then Elmore's leg had hit the front of the bar and he yelped with pain once more. Before he could recover, Wayne hit him hard in the belly, waited as the other bent in the middle, beginning to go down and clasped his hands tightly together, bringing them down hard on the nape of the other's neck. A weaker neck would have broken under the shuddering impact. As it was, the Connaught man uttered a faint bleat of sound and crumpled at Everett's feet, knocked out by the force of the blow.

Even as the other went down, crashing headlong against his knees, Wayne spun for the gunbelt on the top of the counter, knowing that the two men standing near the bar would go for their own guns the instant they saw their champion knocked out. His fingers closed over the butt of the Colt and he spun quickly, then relaxed, saw that he need not have bothered. While the two gunslingers had been intent on watching the fight, Errol had plucked up his courage and snatched the scattergun from its place under the counter. Now he held it on the two men, covering them both. Slowly, his fingers trembling a little, Everett buckled his gunbelt on, straightened up with a jerk and rubbed his jaw tenderly. His chest hurt and it felt as if a couple of ribs had been broken or badly bruised.

But he gave little outward sign of his hurts as he picked up the whisky bottle where it had been placed for Elmore, poured out a glass and tossed it back quickly, grimacing a little as the raw liquor hit the back of his throat. But it brought life back into his battered body and he was able to stand up straight and look about him through rapidly clearing vision.

'Reckon you'd better pick up your wagon boss and haul him out of here,' he said in a harsh voice. 'Next time I see him, I'm liable to plug him right off.' The anger was still surging deep within him, edging his voice with tension.

'You're finished in Yuma,' snarled Torro. His darkly handsome features were contorted. 'This territory won't be big enough for you to hide in when Quentin brings in the Morenci Kid to take care of *hombres* like you.'

'Seems to me that he's been a long time on the trail,' Everett said calmly. 'Could be that he's scared to come.'

'Just keep thinkin' that if it's any real comfort to you,' growled the other. He bent, motioned to his companion and between them they lifted the unconscious form of Bat Elmore and carried him from the saloon.

Errol lowered the shotgun, placed the whisky bottle in front of Wayne. 'This one is on the house,' he said genially. 'You look as though you could use it. Guess that's the first time in many years that anyone has beaten Bat Elmore.'

'Thanks.' Everett sipped the drink slowly this time, fingered the trickle of blood that oozed from the corner of his mouth.

Bat Elmore came round sharply as a pailful of ice-cold water was thrown on to his upturned face. Gasping and spluttering, he pushed himself up on to his arms, shook his head and peered through blurred vision at the men standing over him.

Earl Quentin's sharp voice cut through the roaring in his ears. 'All right, goddammit, get on your feet. You're no use to me lyin' there like a hog.'

Sullenly, as memory came flooding back to him, Elmore scrambled to his feet. The blood rushed pounding through his head and for a moment, he could scarcely stand. Through the sodden thickness of his thoughts, he recalled what had happened in the saloon and a surge of anger beat through his mind. Clenching his fists by his sides, he swung on Quentin.

'That goddamn Everett,' he said through his smashed lips. 'I'll kill him for this. I'll—'

'You'll do exactly as I say,' snapped Quentin. He gripped the other by the arm, fingers clamped on the wagonmaster's flesh. 'Any score you have to settle with Everett you'll do later and in your own time. Right now, you're workin' for me – or maybe you've already forgotten that. It's only half an hour off midnight. Time to destroy those wagons in the Overland yard. Torro and Faro will go with you. And I want no mistakes this time.'

Grabbing up his hat, Elmore punched it back into shape, clamped it on top of his dripping head. With slow care, he moved out of the alley where he had been brought. Torro and Faro followed him, out into the main street, quiet and deserted now. The dust dragged up under their feet. Faro carried a couple of cans of oil.

Working their way along the quayside, they hugged the dark shadows as they approached the Overland Freighting Company's premises. Elmore, thinking a little more clearly now, halted them while they were still thirty yards away. 'They're sure to have a look-out posted near the front gates.' His voice was a low, husky whisper. 'Besides, they'll have 'em locked for certain. We'll get around to the back. There are a couple of loose boards where we can git in.'

Silently, they drifted through the cool darkness of a narrow alley, finished up at the rear of the buildings. Nothing moved apart from a mangy cat which glided from a pool of shadow, eyes gleaming agate-green in the dimness. Feeling his way along the wooden fence that marked off the rear of the long yard, Elmore gave a faint grunt of satisfaction a few moments later.

'This is it,' he murmured. There was a slight creak as he eased the long strip of wood to one side, swinging it around the rusted nail which still held it in place. The adjoining plank was treated in the same manner, making a narrow opening through which they squeezed.

As Faro made to go forward, pointing with his free hand towards the tall shapes of the wagons drawn up in a double line, Elmore stopped him roughly.

'Stay here while I fix the guard,' he ordered in a low tone. Taking his Colt from the holster, where it had been replaced sometime while he had been lying unconscious, he glided into the dimness, a faintly-seen, noiseless shadow. Moving from one wagon to the next, he made his way towards the double gates, crouched down as he saw the slight movement less than fifteen feet away.

The look-out was not as alert as he should have been. Elmore waited for several seconds, watching as the other moved back and forth behind the gates, occasionally slapping his arms around him as the chill air swirled about his body. Getting his feet under him, he waited for a long moment, poised for action, then thrust himself forward, padding catlike behind the other. Some sixth instinct seemed to warn the other of his danger for he whirled while Elmore was still six feet away, his hand dropping towards the gun in its holster. Too late he saw the upraised arm, the gun clubbing down at him. The yell of warning never passed his lips. The heavy butt struck him soggily behind the ear and he fell forward, would have crashed to the ground had Elmore not caught him as he went down, lowering his body to the dirt. Replacing his gun, he went back to where Faro and Torro were waiting, crouched in the shadows. There was a narrow grin on his face as he said: 'That's the guard fixed. Now get out there and do what you have to do.

Start two or three of the wagons goin and the blaze will spread to the others.'

Not wishing to go back to the hotel with his face bruised and bloodied, Wayne Everett had made his way down to the Overland yards a little after eleven o'clock that night and picked himself out a place in the low-roofed building at the rear. There was plenty of straw there, just as comfortable as far as he was concerned as any pillow bed. It was not only this which had prompted him to come here and sleep close to the wagons for the night. The nagging little suspicion of impending trouble was still there in his mind; and the ruckus in the saloon with Bat Elmore had troubled him more than the actual physical pain which had come of it.

Even while he had been fighting the Connaught wagonmaster, there had been the feeling that the other had provoked the fight deliberately, believing that he would emerge the eventual victor, that he could make certain Wayne Everett was in no physical condition to interfere in any work the Connaught crew had planned for the night. Even though Bat Elmore had lost the fight, he had the growing conviction that something was due to happen before the morning. Once the wagon train was on the trail, the chances of hitting it hard would diminish with every passing hour. Here, however, the wagons were particularly vulnerable to attack.

He had washed off most of the dirt and blood at the pump before settling down for the night, intending to remain awake in case of trouble. But the bruising he had received had drained most of the strength from his body and the instant his head touched the straw, he was asleep.

He came awake after what seemed only minutes. The part of his mind that never slept had stirred at some sound in the deep stillness of the night, jerking him back to full consciousness. Gently, he pushed himself up into a sitting position, listened for the sound to repeat itself. When it did not come, he reached out for the Colt lying in its holster beside him, spun the chamber quietly, then got to his feet and moved to the door.

The sky was clear overhead, the stars glittering brilliantly against the dark velvet of the heavens and there was a thin slice of yellow moon, low down in the east, giving a little light to add to the glow of the starshine. Standing there, in the doorway, he strained his senses, peering into the dimness which lay across the yard. The feeling of danger was now stronger than ever before. He waited, cautious and silent, not sure of what was before him. Narrowing his eyes, he tried to make out the prowling figure of the man who was supposed to be near the street gates keeping guard. There was no sign of him. He let the silence drag, grew weary of it, moved carefully out into the yard.

The sudden scrape of a boot on the ground jerked his head around, the gun in his right hand following the movement of his head. He listened to the sound carefully, placed its source somewhere along the further line of wagons, almost halfway to the gate. He heard at last a faintly muttered oath and a long sigh. It was the sudden need for air that had given away the other's position.

There was the metallic clatter of metal on one of the wagon wheels and a gurgle as of liquid being poured from some container. Immediately it came to him. Whoever was out there was trying to fire the wagons. Dropping on to his stomach behind the nearest wagon, he peered upwards, so as to catch the silhouette of anyone out there outlined against the sky. Almost at once, his eyes now accustomed to the darkness, he saw the three huddled shapes. Swiftly, he brought up the gun, finger tightening on the trigger as he lined it up on the nearest of the three.

'Hold it right there,' he called harshly.

Somebody sucked in a long, heavy gust of wind. Then muzzle light leapt blue-crimson at him from the darkness and a slug tore a strip of wood from one of the spokes of the wheel. Instinctively, he fired back, heard a yell grow in the night as his bullet found its mark. He aimed again, saw the brief flare as one of the men struck a sulphur match and tossed it, flaming, into the back of the wagon. There was an immediate orange glow leaping up behind the canvas. Silhouetted against it, he saw the three men, recognised Elmore's bulky form. He fired once more, saw one of the men stumble and clutch at his shoulder, almost falling back into the flames that roared behind him.

'Let's get out of here,' called Elmore's voice above the racket of gunfire.

A volley of bullets hammered around Everett as the others made their move. He caught a brief glimpse of them fading into the shadows that lay around the rim of light thrown by the burning wagon.

Squirming round, Wayne threw a couple more shots at the fleeing men. By the time he had got to his feet they had vanished into the gloom and he knew it would be useless to try to pursue them. At the moment, the immediate need was to put out this fire and prevent it from spreading to the other wagons.

By now, the racketing din of gunfire had alerted the rest of the men and they came running into the yard.

'How did this happen?' asked Elston breathlessly, tucking his shirt into the top of his trousers.

'Some of Quentin's men,' Wayne said quickly. 'I interrupted 'em, otherwise there would be more wagons burnin'.'

Without waiting for a reply from the other, he clambered on top of the burning wagon, feeling the heat searing his face and hands as he grabbed a length of the canvas and began beating out the flames.

Elston clambered up beside him and together they fought the blaze. By now, aided by the oil, the fire had a firm hold, was spreading swiftly to the stores which had been stacked in the back. Little rivulets of burning oil ran along the tongue of the wagon and dripped hissing on to the ground. Within minutes, it was clear to Wayne that they did not have a chance in hell of extinguishing this blaze. The vital thing now, to his way of thinking, was to get the wagon away from the others before the fire could spread and try to save as much of the cargo in the back as possible.

Grabbing Elston by the arm, he yelled: 'Get down and help me drag the wagon away from the others before they all go.'

The other nodded in quick understanding, his sweat-streaming face ruddy in the fiery glow. Swiftly, he dropped to the ground, grabbed at one of the thick wooden shafts as Wayne took hold of the other. More men were running into the yard now, wakened by the smell of smoke and the yells of the others. It seemed scarcely credible to Everett that only a minute or so had passed since he had fired on Bat Elmore and his sidekicks. Now they were temporarily forgotten in the urgent need for action in controlling the blaze.

Straining every muscle, he heaved forward on the shaft with all of his strength. Sweat broke out anew on his body. Jeb Kirby, running forward out of the darkness added his weight to the effort. Slowly at first, then with an increasing momentum, the huge Murphy wagon began to roll forward out of the line. The blistering heat singed the back of Wayne's neck, the crackle of the licking flames was a dull roaring in his skull, almost indistinguishable from the thunder of his own blood beating incessantly behind his temples.

At the end of the yard, Mary Vender showed, her face white and set in the glow. She had started the hand pump, bringing up water from the well and buckets were being filled and passed along a human chain to the burning wagon.

Wayne yelled hoarsely to one of the men nearby, pointed at the bucket the other held. 'Douse me with that; and hurry!'

For a second, the other stared at him in surprise, not comprehending, then recognised that he was in deadly earnest. He flung the contents of the bucket over Wayne. Spluttering under the shock of the ice-cold water hitting him in the face, Wayne brushed the wet tendrils of hair out of his eyes with the back of his hand and climbed back into the wagon. Tendrils of flame licked at his legs. In spite of the soaking he had just received, he could feel his flesh beginning to burn.

The fire was all around him now as he staggered towards the back of the wagon. Smoke rolled out to meet him, getting down into his throat and lungs, threatening to choke him. He could not make out any details. All that existed there in front of him was a mass of fire that roared up the dry canvas stretched tight across the banded steel struts. One or two of the wooden barrels were already smouldering. Grabbing the bowie knife from his belt, he slashed through the tough ropes holding them in place. Brushing an arm across his eyes to ward off the searing heat of the flames, he grabbed the nearest barrel, rolled it to the edge of the wagon and waited as Kirby and Elston manhandled it to the ground.

Turning, he forced himself to go back. His clothing was steaming now as the inferno heat drove all of the water from the cloth. Soon, he would have to drop to the ground if he was not to be roasted alive. In this moment, as he grasped the second barrel, he had his first clear flash of thought since he had clambered back into the wagon. He had started something here that was going to take a good deal of doing. Sheer animal courage was not going to be enough, not nearly enough! Here he would need every bit of luck he had and quick thinking as well as every last ounce of his physical resources. And if it wasn't possible for him to wring a sufficient total out of all that, then this was surely the finish!

His face twisted and convulsed with the effort, he succeeded in getting half a dozen of the barrels out of the wagon before the flames forced him to retreat. He half fell to the ground, knees sagging under him, scarcely able to draw in a breath. His lungs felt as though they, too, were on fire, burned by the superheated air and smoke he had been forced to breathe. The effort to drag the cool night air down into his chest was a harsh and laboured rasping in his throat. His eyes, strained and bloodshot from the continual superhuman effort, seemed fixed in a straight-ahead stare. Blinking them several times, he felt the lids move painfully and dryly over his eyeballs. It felt as if a layer of grit had formed over them, abrading them each time he blinked.

Mary Vender came forward as Elston held him up, his huge arms gripping him around the waist. He was almost naked to the waist. His shirt hung in blackened tatters around his body, flapping across his chest where livid welts showed on the bruised flesh that was streaked and slimed with sweat and blood. He looked like a man who had been clawed and mauled by some great mountain cat.

'Here,' Kirby held out the canteen to him, 'take a drink of this.'

Weakly, Everett tilted it to his lips. It was water, cool and clear. It went down his throat like wine and he could not recall when he had ever tasted anything quite so good. Lowering the canteen, he gave a long, shuddering sigh and leaned against the nearby wagon, one arm over his face. Reaching down, he fumbled for the pocket of his shirt for the makings of a cigarette, then the move stopped short and he lowered his gaze in stunned surprise, amazed to find that he had no shirt. He pondered this strange and inexplicable fact for a moment, then mumbled something under his breath.

'Wayne!' said Mary Vender loudly. She stood in front of him, caught him by the arm. 'Wayne! Can you hear me?'

Weakly, he lifted his head and stared at her. For a moment, he showed no awareness of her presence, then he nodded his head slowly.

'You're going to be all right. I've sent someone for the doctor.

'Still some crates in there,' he muttered.

'Leave them. We can't save them all. I don't want anyone getting himself killed just for the sake of a handful of stores.'

He ran the tip of his tongue around his lips. 'It was Bat Elmore and two of the Connaught crew,' he said tonelessly. 'I heard somethin' and came for a look-see. They must've knocked out the guard. Didn't see him at all.'

'He was hit on the head,' said the girl bitterly. 'I guess he wasn't quite as alert as you were. It's all due to you that we've managed to save the other wagons. There's no doubt they intended to destroy them all.'

'You still intendin' to push them out tomorrow, Miss Vender?' asked Kirby quietly.

She nodded determinedly. 'We'll go ahead on schedule. Every man will have to be armed in case they try again. After tonight, my guess is that Quentin will stop at nothing.'

Wayne rubbed his hand over his face. 'I'll get washed up,' he said. 'Only a few more hours and–'

'I want you to stay here in town, Wayne,' Mary Vender spoke sharply, her tone a little defiant, as though she knew he would argue. 'For a couple of days at least.'

He stared at her in surprise. 'This is nothin',' he said tightly. 'Ain't no need for a doctor. Just a few bruises and blisters that'll heal up on the trail as well as in town.'

She showed him an expression that meant nothing to him, then said frankly: 'That isn't why I want you here. If the Morenci Kid does ride into town in response to Quentin's message, I want someone here I can trust. If he doesn't arrive in the next two days, then I shall want you to ride out with a couple of the men and follow the trail north-west, shadow the wagon train. That way, you should be in a position to stop any trouble that might develop on the way.'

Her tone brooked no argument. Even Wayne was forced to admit that the plan had its merits. He thought the whole thing over very carefully as he stood there, feeling the cold night air on his face.

5

ACT OF DANGER

Watching the long wagon train moving out along the main street of Yuma, Wayne Everett's mood was one of sombre bitterness. Over and over in his mind ran the thought that his stay here in town was a big mistake, could even be playing into Quentin's hands. By now, the other would certainly have known that he had not ridden out with the train. What would Quentin do now? The facts he knew were callous and ugly. They told of a schemed plan of murder and plunder, of the avaricious desire for power and wealth.

He fingered his face, still painful where the flames had seared across it. Building a smoke, he lit the cigarette and stood leaning against the wooden upright. The last of the cumbersome wagons vanished around the corner of the street, leaving the white irritating dust to settle slowly. Wayne stared at the spot for several moments, then turned to make his way back to the Overland offices.

He experienced a feeling of impotent help-lessness and because this was a new sensation to him, he did not like it. He wished now that he had argued with Mary Vender, forcing her to let him go with the others.

The Morenci Kid would not arrive on the stage today, or any other day as Quentin had threatened. The Connaught boss knew that; but he probably also knew that even the mere threat of the Kid's impending arrival was enough to force Mary Vender's hand and keep him here in town.

Glancing across the street, he stiffened abruptly as the doors of the saloon opposite were thrust open and Bat Elmore stepped on to the boardwalk. The tall wagonmaster gave a quick look up and down the street, saw Wayne standing there and walked slowly and purposefully over, his thumbs stuck into his gunbelt. He paused when he was a few feet away. Over the other's shoulder, Wayne saw two more of the Connaught rannies troop out of the saloon and follow until they stood on either side of Elmore, a little to the rear.

Grinning mockingly, Elmore said: 'You look as if you've been in some kind of trouble, Everett. Guess workin' for the

Overland just don't agree with you. Still, you can't say I didn't warn you. Pity you didn't listen to me.'

Wayne clenched his teeth tightly together as he let his gaze wander slowly from one mocking face to another, but his tone was calm and even as he replied: 'Wasn't any trouble we couldn't handle, Bat. When we find snakes slidin' around durin' the night, we stomp on 'em.'

He felt a thrill of satisfaction as he saw the murderous gleam that came into the other's eyes, glinting redly in their depths. Then Elmore had himself under a tight rein once more. 'We heard there was a fire last night.' He shrugged. 'Somebody gettin' a mite careless?'

'Could be,' Wayne nodded. 'Though one of 'em stopped a bullet for his pains.'

Elmore's features sharpened. 'You insinuatin' we started that fire, Everett?' His tone had become high and threatening.

'Sure. I saw you myself. It was me who put a bullet into your friend.'

'Reckon it's your word against mine, Everett. Trouble is, nobody knows your background here in Yuma, except that you're probably a fast gun from somewhere down south and I can prove where I was all last night.'

Wayne's voice was sarcastic. 'You could bring in a score of men to say you weren't within a dozen miles of Yuma and the Overland yard last night and it still wouldn't make any difference.'

'You callin' me a liar?' Elmore's tone was challenging. He took a couple of deliberate steps backward towards the middle of the street, his hands hovering just above the butts of the guns at his waist. 'Guess I shall have to do somethin' about that.'

Wayne stepped clear of the wooden upright at the edge of the boardwalk to give his gunhand freedom of movement. Eyes narrowed down, he watched the three Connaught men with an unfocused gaze. In those seconds everything seemed curiously magnified for him; objects appeared enlarged to more than twice their normal size and he could hear the faintest sounds clearly, a horse down the street chomping impatiently on its bit, the noises from the quayside in the distance where the river moved sluggishly through the town.

Tension crackled in the stillness that held over the street. It needed only the slightest untoward movement to set guns talking. Wayne was not sure that he could take all three men with him before he went down, if the two rannies decided to back Elmore's play; but he would have a good try. From the way they had stepped out a little on either side of the wagonmaster to split his fire, he reckoned they meant to take him from three sides.

Then, abruptly, the spell was broken. A buckboard came around the corner, thirty yards away with Mary Vender sitting tall and erect on the high seat. At almost the same moment, Doc Harding stepped up along the boardwalk beside Wayne. He said in a quiet, casual tone: 'Must you always go meetin' trouble more than halfway, young fella?'

'Stay out of this, Doc. It doesn't concern you.' Wayne said sharply.

'Sure, sure.' The other ignored his warning, came right up to him, leaned against the upright. He took a thin black cigar from his pocket and lit it as if he was merely having a casual talk about the weather and had not moved into the middle of an impending gunfight. 'Makes no difference to me, I suppose, if you stand there and get yourself murdered, even though I did lose half my sleep last night patchin' you up. But I don't like to see a fight that's so loaded it's sheer cold-blooded murder.'

Grimly Wayne said: 'Even if I don't take all three of these critters, Doc, Elmore knows he'll be the first to stop a bullet and nothin' his men can do will save him from that.'

'Better take a look on the roof of the grain store across the street,' Harding said softly. 'That *hombre* there with the rifle is all set to pick you off the minute you go for your gun. Sure, it'll look as if you drew first, but you'll be dead before you can pull the trigger.'

Carefully, Wayne cocked a quick glance at the flat roof opposite. As Harding had said, there was a man crouched there, the long barrel of the Winchester gleaming bluely in the harsh glare of the sunlight, and pointed directly at his chest. The flame of anger roared through his mind again, so intense that it was difficult for him to try to control it. The thought of action was strong in him, to draw on Elmore and be done with it, in spite of that gun which dominated everything.

Then he lowered his gaze, saw the expression of fury on Bat Elmore's face, saw the other shift his stance slightly as if ready to go for his gun in spite of Doc Harding's warning.

'If I were you, Elmore,' Harding said, his

voice strangely hushed. 'I'd turn around and walk away while you're still on your feet. Miss Vender still has some friends in Yuma apart from those who rode out with the wagons. Better make sure there aren't any rifles trained on you.'

'You're bluffin', Harding,' growled the other. But even as he spoke, his glance slid uneasily from one side of the boardwalk to the other. Then his hands moved well away from his sides as he noticed the men who stood in the doorways and at the open windows of the stores. Wayne turned and saw them, too. About eight of them, each man with a rifle or shotgun, ordinary citizens of Yuma, but ready to back Mary Vender against these men.

Savagely, Elmore muttered something to the two men, spun on his heel and walked back to the saloon. Lifting his head, Wayne saw that the marksman on the roof opposite had also vanished.

Standing just inside the door of the office, his hat in his hands, Wayne observed the look of concern on the girl's face as she paced the room nervously.

'There's somethin' wrong, Mary?' he asked quietly.

'Perhaps. One of the boys rode in a little while ago. Seems that a stranger got on the stage at Los Lobos this morning. From the description I got of him, it could be the Morenci Kid.'

Wayne mused over this for a while, then said harshly. 'If it is, we'll soon know. Quentin will be meetin' the stage when it gets here. I'll keep an eye on things.'

She eyed him speculatively for a while, held her silence for a matter of minutes, then asked directly: 'You must have had a reason for wanting to join the Overland, Wayne. What was it?'

He countered with: 'Does a man always have to have a reason for what he does?'

'Not every time, perhaps. But when it comes to a stranger riding into town and deliberately turning down the offer to join the most powerful outfit, then coming over to this one, knowing that I can't possibly pay the wages that Earl Quentin does, and knowing that there will only be trouble and danger so long as you work for me, I think there must be a reason. Just who are you, Wayne? What are you doing here in Yuma?' Her brows were drawn together a little as she watched his face, trying to read some of the answers there; failing to gain anything from the guarded look.

'Just a drifter, nothin' more,' he said casually. 'As for why I didn't take up Bat Elmore's offer, that's easily explained. I didn't like the man when I first met him and what I've seen both of him and Quentin has reaffirmed my judgment of them. I'm choosey as to who I work for. Besides, maybe I like to help the underdog. I've seen too many cases of big men movin' in and takin' over everythin'. This frontier is never goin' to change until there's fair competition.'

Her gaze was still narrowed and wondering, seeing him with grave eyes. Then she said: 'Wayne, just how old are you?'

He smiled a little at that. 'Twenty-seven,' he said softly. 'But right now, after last night, I feel twice that age.'

'Sometimes I get the feeling you're bitter about something. Almost as if there's something in your past that you're running away from; yet to me you don't look like the ordinary kind of trail-jumper we get around here. There's something much more to your character than that.'

'I hope you'll stay with your judgment,' he said enigmatically.

'Then there is something.' Immediately she spoke, she knew that it was the wrong thing to say and went on quickly: 'I'm sorry, Wayne. I know I don't have the right to ask that. Please forgive me and forget I asked it.'

His smile widened a little. 'It's already forgotten.'

'Please remember that if there is ever anything I can do to help, you have only to ask. Far too often, men have come to work here first for my father and then for me, only to drift away when the going became tough. It's pleasing to find someone who will remain loyal. But I wish that you didn't hate things so much. I hate to see much bitterness in a man'

He nodded slowly, tried to answer that and could not. Lifting his hat, he said: 'Time to go. I reckon.'

'Where?'

'I think I'll take a walk along to the stage depot, see what's going on there.' He waited a moment, then went on: 'I still figure it's dangerous to let the wagon train go on and keep me here in Yuma.'

She said: 'I know how you feel about that. If the Morenci Kid isn't on the stage, or if he is, and Quentin sends him and his men after the train, then I want you to ride out with Slim and Yarrow. It may do no good, I don't know. But this is the last stand that the

Overland can make. Fail now, and it will be the end. The bank has already decided that they won't advance a further loan to tide me over the next trip.'

'That will be Quentin's doing. He's too friendly with George Frew.'

'I know.' Lowering herself into the chair, she sat with her elbows on the table, staring straight in front of her, shoulders slumped a little. For a moment, watching her sitting there, seemingly so helpless, Wayne wanted to take her into his arms, comfort her, tell her that everything would come all right in the end.

He walked over to her, saw the way her mouth struggled to hold its tight, firm shape and then eventually come loose. She wanted to cry, to let it all out in a flood of tears and only her indomitable will was holding her together. He put his arm around her, felt her body tremble and the tears come, dropping warm on to the back of his hand. Holding her tightly, knowing the misery in her, realising all that it must have taken these past months since her father had been killed, for the first time in many years, he felt pity for another human being. Always in the past he had been so self-reliant, had hated to see weakness in anyone else, knowing that it was not in him. But this was somehow different. She rested her head against his shoulder and kept it there for several moments, then pulled herself upright, wiped the back of her hand over her eyes, checking her crying.

'I'm sorry, I'm all right now, Wayne.' Getting to her feet, she walked over to the window, stared out over the town. 'I know I oughtn't to hate this town, but there are times when I feel there is nothing else I can do. It has brought nothing but pain and misery to me for so long. We came here full of hopes, wanting only to be left alone to work out our own destinies. But we were denied that. My father had to die because he had principles and tried to distinguish between what was right and what was wrong. I thought that maybe I could carry on, I was so determined to do so because I knew it would be what he would have wanted. But over the past few weeks things have been building up to a head, with everything working against me and now it seems I can't go on any further.'

'You'll go on all the way to the end, Mary,' he said with conviction. 'There are shallow people who run at the first sign of danger; and there are those others who have unplumbed depths of strength and character so that they can always find a reserve of determination and courage even when things look their darkest. You're one of those women, Mary; and never let anyone tell you otherwise.'

She blinked away the last of her tears and smiled bravely at him. 'Thanks, Wayne. You'll never know how much you've helped me this morning. Now you'd better go along to the stage depot. Don't worry about me. I'll be all right. But if the Morenci Kid does step off that stage, be careful.'

He grinned back at her. 'I'll be careful,' he said meaningly.

Reaching the stage depot, Wayne Everett stationed himself in the shade thrown by the wide overhang on the opposite side of the street from where he would be able to watch all of the comings and goings without being too conspicuous himself. Apart from this consideration, the heat thrown back from the dusty surface of the street was hotter than the hinges of hell, scorching in shimmering waves through the sunlight. Even the air that he dragged down into his lungs seemed to have been pulled through some gigantic inferno before it had reached the town.

Ten minutes before the stage was due, Earl Quentin rode up in a buckboard, halted it a short distance along the street and sat back on the high seat, occasionally pulling out a large red handkerchief and mopping his sweating face. He looked ill-at-ease and impatient, sometimes lifting himself a little in the seat, staring off along the road where it wound out of town and towards the desert that lay to the east. Wayne watched him fidget, wondered what thoughts were passing through the other man's mind at that moment. Was he actually expecting someone in off the stage? He rolled himself a cigarette, lit it and smoked it slowly. There were few other men on the street. The heat head was so intense it had driven others to seek what shade they could find.

The sound of horses in the distance stirred him from his frowning reverie. The stage came in a cloud of dust, visible at first on the skyline a mile or so away, but coming nearer swiftly as if both driver and horses were anxious to reach town. Thrusting himself away from the wall, Wayne dropped his cigarette butt on to the ground and rubbed it out with his heel. In the buckboard, Earl Quentin had half risen to

144

his feet. In the harsh glare of sunlight there was visible the tight pressure around his lips and the impatience locked up behind his eyes.

With a creaking rattle, the stage pulled up outside the depot and the man riding shotgun clambered down, went around and opened the door, pulling down the steps. Two women got out first, paused for a moment, glancing round at Quentin who had got out of the buckboard and was walking quickly forward along the far boardwalk.

Then there was a pause and the third passenger alighted. Wayne eyed him narrowly, tried to search his memory for any recognition of the other's face, but found nothing. The man was a stranger to him; short and slender, plainly-dressed, with a black hat on the back of his head. He wore his gunbelt beneath a frock coat, the Colts showing briefly as he moved. He caught the grip that the driver dropped down to him, made to go towards the depot, then looked round as Quentin came up to him and said something urgently in a low undertone. A moment later, the two of them walked to the waiting buckboard, got in and Quentin drove off, slashing the whip across the horse's back, urging it forward at a smart trot.

'You reckon that was the Morenci Kid, Wayne?'

He turned at the voice. Yarrow stood watching the departing buckboard with a worried gaze. 'Seems like those two knew each other anyway, whoever he was.'

'He had all the makings of a gunfighter,' Wayne admitted. 'Funny though that Quentin met him like this, almost as if he didn't want anyone in town to know that his man had arrived.'

Yarrow pursed his lips. 'What you got on your mind, Wayne?'

'I'm not sure yet. But for a week now, Quentin has been threatenin' us with the Morenci Kid. I'd have expected him to make a big thing out of this, make sure that everyone in town knew he was here. Instead of that, he meets him like a couple of rustlers in the night.'

'Guess he must have his reasons.' He scratched his bristly chin. 'Better let Miss Vender know. She can decide then if we're to ride out after the train.'

'Well, Wayne?' Mary Vender asked as he walked into the office a quarter of an hour later. Anxiety sharpened her tone more than she had intended.

'Quentin met someone off the stage,' he said simply. 'It could have been the Morenci Kid, but I doubt it.'

'Did he look like a – gunslinger?' She spoke the word with distaste.

'He sure looked a mean cuss,' Yarrow spoke up from the doorway. 'He carried guns, too, like he meant to use 'em if he ever got the chance.'

'Then he could have been the Morenci Kid?'

'If he is,' said Yarrow positively, 'then you can stake your last dollar that Quentin has got him here for only one purpose. Not to shoot things out with Wayne here, though I figure that could happen if Wayne was to try to stop Quentin here in Yuma; but to lead his men against the wagon train. If they were to light out of town this afternoon, they could overtake the wagons in a day or so and you can guess what that will mean.'

Mary was silent for several moments. She had been studying Wayne's face all the time with a critical gaze and what she saw there brought the worry back to her own features again. She had half lifted her right hand, but now she let it fall limply to her side.

'I've the feeling that I sent those men out to their deaths,' she said dully. 'This must be what Quentin was waiting for.' She looked appealingly at Wayne. He knew what was on her mind; knew what she was trying to say.

'How many men do you think that Quentin can muster?'

'Twenty at least, possibly thirty.'

'And it's more'n likely he'll send out every one of them just to be sure there's no mistake.' He threw a quick look at Yarrow. 'Reckon we'd better be ready to move out at sundown. We can make good time through the night though it would be safer if we stayed off the main trails and headed across country.'

The girl looked at him with a moment's penetrating attention. 'Do you know that desert out there, Wayne?'

'Nope. But I reckon it's no different from that to the east.'

'Could be. There are waterholes along the main trail north but once you get off it, you could find yourself in trouble. It's been a long, dry summer. Most of the smaller holes will have dried up.'

'That's a risk we'll have to take, Mary,' he said seriously. 'I aim to trail the wagon train, keepin' a little way behind, but off the trail itself, so we have a chance of jumpin' Quentin's men if they attack, split their fire.'

With thirty men to face, even that was not too hopeful, he reminded himself; but in circumstances like this, they had to get every bit of edge on to their sides that they could.

The main street was an empty, lonely place shortly after sundown that evening, in spite of the blazing yellow lights that tunnelled into the darkness from the doors and windows of the saloon. Off along the street, the water of the Colorado River washed leadenly against the wooden piles of the quay and from somewhere along the river, the low melancholy blast of a river steamer's siren sounded in the stillness.

The nearest saloon was full as Earl Quentin thrust open the doors with the flat of his hand and went inside, the frock-coated gunman walking close on his heels. The tinny jingle of the piano in the corner was half drowned by the roar of voices and the clink of the glasses and coins on the tables as the faro and poker games got under way for the evening. As Earl Quentin paused just inside the doorway, squinting his eyes against the glaring yellow light, some of the noise ebbed. A few heads were turned in his direction, looked aside at the man who stood half behind him, then slid cautiously away as though they were afraid to meet the narrowed gaze of the gunman accompanying him. Earl sauntered slowly over to the bar. A couple of men made way for him, but even so he roughly shouldered one of them aside, knocking the man off balance. A faint grin split his features as he watched the man slink off, his face sullen, but his eyes downcast.

Silence clamped down tightly in the saloon now. Quentin turned casually away from the bar once the whisky bottle had been brought and set in front of him, surveying the crowd there. Most of his men, he noticed, were there as he had ordered, sitting in on the card games, or lounging against the bar at the far end. After a couple of drinks, he moved over to one of the empty tables and signalled all of his men over. Crowding around the table, they stood waiting.

'Boys. This is the *hombre* I told you about,' he said, nodding towards the gunman seated beside him. 'He got into town this mornin'. A little late, but through no fault of his. Now he's here, we can go after that

Overland wagon train. My guess is they can't be more'n fifty miles ahead of us. If we light out of town tonight, we should sight 'em sometime tomorrow afternoon, maybe before that if they stop to make long camp tonight.'

'From what I hear, I reckon they'll push on as fast as they can for the nearest Army post, try to get rid of some of their supplies before we hit 'em,' said Torro Mendez. 'Mary Vender is no fool. She'll have guessed by now that we're behind all of this trouble and we'll have to trail 'em now.'

'So they push on,' growled Quentin. He lit a cigar, puffed the smoke into the air over his head. 'That won't help 'em none. With those wagons they can't make much more than thirty miles a day at best and the Badlands out there are a treacherous place.'

Mendez scowled as if he didn't understand or didn't agree. Hands hanging loosely by his sides, he spoke up again: 'And when we do catch up with 'em. What then? Do we finish them off altogether?'

Quentin stared at him sharply, lips drawn tight around the cigar. 'You know what my orders are, Torro. I don't want any of that wagon train to get through to the Army posts. If you can kill the men with it and still save most of the wagons and supplies, then fair enough. If not, then destroy everythin'.'

'The Kid ridin' out with us?' asked Cal Fenner.

'We're both coming. We'll be a short ways behind the rest of you.'

For a moment, some answer seemed poised on Fenner's mind, then he swallowed thickly and tightened his lips, watching Earl Quentin through narrowed, empty eyes.

Either Quentin did not trust them to carry out his orders properly, or as was more likely, he did not want to risk his own skin by riding with them and attacking the wagon train. He felt a momentary anger against the other, then thrust it away with an effort. With the Morenci Kid backing him, it would be both stupid and foolish to try to make anything of it. He let his glance wander in the direction of the Kid again, noticing the pale features, thin and pinched almost to the point of gauntness, the slender, white fingers on top of the table. The eyes were grey and cold, flecked a little with red. A tough and dangerous customer in spite of his deceptive appearance. He felt a little chill go through him. There was a man he would not have liked to tangle with.

Earl Quentin finished half of the bottle of

whisky, then got heavily to his feet, consulted the watch he pulled from his pocket, the chain glinting brightly in the lantern light.

'Right, boys, get saddled up. We're movin' out. Take plenty of water and ammunition. It's goin' to be mighty dry out there.'

The Connaught outfit moved in a bunch towards the door. A few moments later they were gone and at the bar, Flint Errol, pouring a drink for one of the rivermen, said harshly: 'I wouldn't like to be on the receivin' end of those boys. They're in an ugly mood and they sure mean business.'

'They ridin' out for trouble?' inquired the other hoarsely, slamming down the empty glass.

'Trouble for some folk,' answered the other tonelessly. He went back to polishing the glasses, setting them in a neat row at the back of the counter, fairly certain now that there would be little trouble in the saloon that night, with all of the Connaught men out of town.

Half an hour before the Connaught riders left town, cutting the sign of the wagon train now almost two days ahead of them, Wayne Everett and the two Overland men had ridden out of Yuma. They rode north-west, Wayne showing the way, following the wide trail for almost five miles before they cut off into the darkness of the scrubland which lay to the south. This was the edge of the Badlands, a wilderness of gaunt sky-rearing buttes and mesas, of rocks etched and fluted into weird, fantastic shapes by long geological ages of wind and sand scouring.

The night air was bitterly cold and there was a breeze blowing from the north-west which, although slight, was sufficient to lift some of the fine grains of sand from the crests of the dunes and whip it into their faces, forcing them to ride crouched low in the saddle, heads tucked down, eyes and mouths clamped together.

Slim and Yarrow rode side by side most of the time, a short distance behind Everett, each man engrossed in his own thoughts, trying not to think of what might lie ahead of them once they sighted the Connaught outfit. The ground became rougher as they edged further from the trail, slashed by narrow, but deep crevasses, forcing them to slow their pace for fear of their mounts getting a foot in one of these cracks.

Wayne rode low in the saddle, his straight hatbrim low over his eyes. To the men who rode behind him, he could have been asleep in the saddle, from the loose easy way his body swayed to every motion made by the big stallion; but he was not asleep and his eyes and ears missed nothing.

At their first rest, midway through the early hours of the morning, with only the starlight and the yellow glow that came from a thin yellow scratch of a moon low in the heavens, Wayne walked to a high mound of sand, clambered to the top of it, feet sliding precariously under him in the shifting sand, and peered out into the distance in the direction where he reckoned the main trail to be, straining every sense to pick out the faintest sound and the slightest movement. There was a deep stillness all about him. He heard the faint snicker from one of the horses behind him, but nothing more. Shivering a little in the cold, he sat there for almost ten minutes, not once relaxing his vigilance.

At a rough reckoning, he figured they were the best part of a mile and a half from the trail. At that distance, it would be quite possible to pick out the sound made by a bunch of hard riding men. Finally, when the silence continued, he went back to the others, found them seated beside the horses.

The two men glanced up at him as he approached.

'No sign of them,' he said quietly, in response to the mute inquiry on their faces.

'Maybe they rode out of town before we left,' suggested Slim.

Wayne shook his head. 'They were still in the saloon when we pulled out. I saw Quentin and that gunslinger go in.'

'So they might even have had the same idea as us and be ridin' off the main trail.'

'That's possible,' Wayne admitted. 'Though unlikely. They'll be travellin' fast, hopin' to overtake the train before they hit one of the outposts.'

'They'll do that easily enough,' said Yarrow. He scratched a match on his pants, lit his second cigarette, watched the redly glowing tip in thoughtful concentration.

'How do you know that?' Wayne asked sharply.

'Because I know the territory that's ahead of us,' retorted the other. He pointed a stiff arm to the west. 'Ten miles, maybe even less, and we hit the roughest, hottest, meanest stretch of country you've ever known in your life. There are long stretches of malpais there where the trail is all but obliterated by the blown sand and if your mount happens to step off it for more'n ten minutes, then you can goddamn shoot him, because his feet won't carry him any further.'

'As bad as that?' inquired Wayne.

'You don't know the half of it. Then there's the heat and the glare. It can drive a man mad and blind if he ain't real careful. I've been through it with the wagon trains a dozen times and on each occasion it seems worse than ever. I tell you, Wayne, that's the nearest place to hell on Earth I know.'

'Fifteen miles, you say.'

The other nodded, dragged the sweet-smelling smoke down into his lungs. 'About that, give or take a couple of miles. It's more than twenty miles across, too, with no water-hole that anybody has ever found. Some reckon there's one nearly halfway over, but I ain't never met anyone who's found it.'

'And it'll be daylight when we hit it.' Wayne got to his feet as he spoke, tightened the cinch under the belly of the stallion. 'Let's go.'

Grumbling a little, Slim heaved himself to his feet, climbed into the saddle. Turning their faces to the west they began to ride. Behind them, the moon lifted slightly in the south-east and the utter chill of the desert country settled more deeply on them that even the thought of the warmth that would come at sun-up seemed something to look forward to with promise and anticipation.

The sun, an hour up above the horizon, beat down on the country with a fierce and inextinguishable intensity, drying and burning, sucking all of the moisture from the ground and from the bodies of men and horses with a cruel and relentless strength. Around the three men the heat expanded like some evil blossom, opening its petals to envelop them, already ovenlike. Rubbing the dust from his eyes, drooping in the saddle, Wayne Everett peered about him. Except for the twisting swirls of dust, white and curiously ashy, nothing moved in every direction.

Worry tinged his mind. Since dawn he had searched the flat, limitless horizons, looking for the tell-tale smudge of dust that would give away the position of any large band of riders. But there had been nothing. The glaring sunlight skewed everything in its place. Removing his hat, he wiped the sweat from his forehead, blinking his eyes against the vicious glare.

'This is just the start,' croaked Yarrow. His face was a mask of sweat and dust. He moistened his parched, cracked lips and his crooked eyes stared from beneath low-drawn brows, scanning the shimmering, endless desert.

It was evil, tainted country, a monotonous expanse that seemed to go on for ever, terrible, treacherous and frightening. Since they had entered it, they had seen neither animal or insect, not even a lizard or a rattler. It was as if even they shunned this place. Wayne did not know this country, and he did not like it. As he rode, clothed in heat and glare, his thoughts swirled and drifted in his mind. Earl Quentin and his men were somewhere on the trail. It was a wonder he had not spotted them by now. Here, in the malpais, it was possible to see for more than thirty miles in every direction.

Yarrow gigged his mount forward until he came alongside him. Rubbing his mouth for a moment, he said in a harsh croak. 'Somethin' yonder, Wayne.'

Wayne followed the direction of his hand. There seemed to be no change in the land around them. The same flatness extended everywhere he could see; the same poverty of vegetation, the monotony of yellow and red. Then he saw the small puff of white which lay close to the horizon. It seemed unmoving at that distance and he had to watch it closely for two minutes before he had satisfied himself that it was actually moving.

Then, drawing in a harsh breath which rasped in his throat and burned deep in his lungs, he nodded. 'You're right. It's Quentin and his outfit. It has to be.'

'They're movin' in the right direction,' mused the other, rubbing the bristle of his beard. 'Headin' a little away from us I'd say, off to the north-west.'

'That's where the main trail would be?'

'That's right. This is an old Indian trail we've been followin' since dawn. It links up with the other about eight miles on.'

Wayne pondered that. It meant if they continued on this trail they would lose some ground on those men, but to be counted against this were the facts that they dare not approach too close during the daytime for fear of being seen in this flat country and also, he recalled what Yarrow had said about the effect on the horses if they tried to ride through the malpais, off the trail.

'We'll stick with this route,' he said, reaching a sudden decision. 'But try not to raise dust. We're still close enough to be seen if they should decide to scan behind them.'

'If they should do that they'll be starin' right into the sun,' Slim said. He lifted his canteen, shook it gently close to his ear, listening to the faint splash of the liquid inside. His tongue moved around his cracked lips and his hand half lifted to remove the cork. Then he thought better of it, thrust it half-angrily away.

Twice, in their journey along the Indian trail, they came across small buffalo wallows where it seemed that no rain had fallen for the whole of the year. The earth there was cracked and lanced across by the heat. It crumbled into a fine dust under the hooves of the horses as they trampled across it. Yarrow's lips curled in an expression of disgust. He knocked the dust from his shirt with a savage movement, lips thinned, as if this somehow relieved his feelings. The sun was now reaching up to its zenith, breaking down on them with a savage relentless fury. Goddamn, thought Wayne irritatedly; this could burn and peel the hide off a man in no time at all. Even the thought that Quentin and his men were probably suffering the same discomforts failed to elicit any comfort in his mind. The heat forced silence on the three men as their mounts plodded forward through the dust, heads lowered.

161

The animals seemed to have a mind of their own now and no amount of spurring would force them into any quicker pace. The malpais held them in its terrible grip and as he sat in the saddle, perspiration oozing from every pore, Wayne had the odd feeling that they were three flies pinned down on some flat inferno-heated board, moving aimlessly to an unknown and unguessable destination. Across the burning land, the heat devils shivered and danced. Tall spirals of dust would rise up like ghostly wraiths from the ground, spun around for long seconds, before collapsing to the ground. At times, during the long afternoon, as the trail curved slowly to the north, lakes would shimmer eerily in front of them, smooth sheets of cool water, beckoning them forward; and for a handful of agonising seconds, they would rake spurs along the heaving flanks of their horses, only to see the mirage shiver and fade as they drew nearer.

It was sundown by the time they reached the main trail. Wayne rode ahead of the other two, bent forward in the saddle, eyes searching for sign. He located the tracks of several riders easily. Here and there, the drifting sand had obliterated them, but for the most part the hoofmarks were plain in the dust.

'That's them,' said Yarrow positively, nodded. He stared off into the deep reds and golds flaring in the west where the sun had dropped down behind the horizon like a great red penny going into a black box.

Now there was a decision to be made. Whether to ride fast through the coming night, or to move cautiously. He halted, reining up sharply. Turning to the others, he said: 'We've got us a problem. I figure they passed here a couple of hours ago, not much longer.'

'So we ought to come up on 'em in two or three hours,' muttered Slim.

'And suppose they've stopped and made camp. We'd be on 'em before we knew they were there. That's the last thing I want.'

Yarrow uncorked his canteen and tilted it to his lips, took a mouthful and washed it around his teeth before allowing it to trickle down his throat. 'Then what do we do?'

'I think they'll be inclined to keep movin' until they spot the wagons,' said Wayne after a reflective pause. 'Quentin may be the careful type, but he won't want those wagons to slip through his fingers. He'll never rest until he's destroyed them.'

'Assumin' they stick to the trail, we have no other choice. Keep your eyes and ears open. The horses may give us a warnin' before we stumble on 'em.'

Daylight was almost completely gone when they reached the further edge of the malpais and they followed Quentin's tracks through a waste of scrub and sword grass which slashed at their horses' feet, and then on through a stand of timber which fronted the rimrock. The horses moved more slowly now, more careful, as the slope became steeper, often making switchbacks through the stunted pines which grew more dense as they edged along the narrow ridge which looked down on to the flatness of the desert fifty feet or more below.

Dipping and rolling in long gradual swells of land, the open country soon loomed before them, cool now in the lessening heat of evening. They rode swiftly down the long sweep of rocky ground with the breeze blowing in their faces. Ahead of them, they could just make out sky-rearing, gigantic formations of rock which lifted from the smooth territory, around the bases of the buttes, the irregular boulders lay tumbled in massive heaps through the wild brush of the narrow valley floor.

Heading this way, the wild country would slow Quentin and his men to an appreciable extent. Wayne gestured towards the maze of valleys which opened out in front of them.

'Where do these valleys end?' he asked swiftly.

Yarrow pointed towards the dark green mass of trees on the far rim of the hills. 'There's a pass yonder, about half an hour's ride. Then a quick dip down into the desert again. After that, it's five days' journey to the California border in that direction.'

Then that's the way both the wagon train and Quentin would go, thought Wayne tightly; because there ought to be water there, on this side of the desert, and none of those men knew when they would see it again once they left the hills.

6

GUNMAN'S BLUFF

The desert sun beat down on the wagon train. Time became a tenuous and endless blur of racked throats and tortured lungs. Seated on the stoop of the lead wagon, Jeb Kirby tried to measure it. Ten minutes, fifteen; then half an hour. Endless, stifling, the heat was oppressive, shutting down on a man until he could neither breathe nor think properly. The horses ridden by the outriders and the oxen, hauling the cumbersome wagons, were beginning to feel the heat, too. For the first two days they had been relatively fresh, snatching a few hours rest during the heat of high noon and making up for it at night when travel was a little more bearable, though not much. Then it was the bitter cold that ate at a man's nerves and his tiny reserves of strength, drained him of his energy.

He must be getting old, he reckoned. There had been a time, he recalled, his mind working dully as he tried to remember details, when the old man had been alive, when he had been able to make this trip twice every month and think nothing about it, so long as there was plenty of cool beer waiting for him when he made it back to Yuma.

He flicked his tongue around his parched lips at the thought of beer. He would almost sell his soul to the devil and give up all hope of heaven for just one single glass full of the beer they sold in the saloon at that very moment. Taking a strip of chewing tobacco from his pocket, he stared at it thoughtfully for a long moment, debating whether to bite off a piece, knowing it might take his mind off their troubles for a little while, but that it would soak up all of the moisture which still remained in his mouth, leaving it as cracked and dry as the flesh on his grizzled cheeks. Finally, he put the tobacco away, tried to shift his cramped body into a more comfortable position on the hard wooden seat. The wagon swayed precariously from side to side as first one set of wheels drifted into the loose sand at the edge of the trail and then the other went on. The endless swaying motion brought a dull sense of nausea to the pit of his stomach and the dizzying glare refracted from the sand and rocks on either side was also sickening. He sat up straighter on the seat, fighting off the vertigo.

Matt Elston drifted forward, sitting loosely in the saddle. His features were an angry red from the sun.

'Only another three days of this and we should hit Fort Comanche. Then we can unload half of this load and take on fresh food and water for ourselves. We've still got enough to take us there without trouble, although I had hoped there would have been water at that waterhole back there a piece.'

'Summer's been too bad this year,' grunted Kirby. 'One of the worst droughts I've known in all my years in this territory.'

'I've got some men scoutin' around for signs of trouble.'

'You still reckon Quentin will follow us?'

Elston nodded. 'He'll come,' he said positively. 'Make no mistake about that. He'll come. And when he does, it'll be a fight to the finish. He knows he has to get rid of us all this time. There can't be any witnesses left. The Army will want to know what happened if these supplies don't get through. He may tell 'em that we were jumped by renegade Indians, or maybe outlaws. But whatever story he tells, he can't leave anyone alive to refute him.'

'You reckon Miss Vender knew this when she sent us out?'

'Could be that she had her suspicions, but nothin' more to go on than that.'

'I still get the feelin' I'm just a chicken squattin' with its head laid out on the choppin' block with the axe just about to fall,' grunted the other.

'Stick with that thought,' said the other harshly. 'You may not be so far wrong after all.'

He swung sharply on the reins, pulling his mount's head around, and it was at that precise moment that they caught the first distant break of gunfire. It came from behind them, over to the north, the shots growing in volume, the sound coming down to them through the still air that lay like a smothering blanket over the glaring face of the desert, making soft flutters in the silence.

'Trouble!' Elston snapped harshly. He blinked, peered through the heat haze, staring out of sunken eyes. 'Quentin?'

'Couldn't be anyone else unless one of the boys has run foul of some Indian war party and that ain't likely in these parts. They normally shun the desert like poison.'

Kirby whipped the oxen savagely, striving to urge them on at a faster pace, but the long hours on the trail had taken its toll of even their strength and they could manage little more than a flagging motion, the axles of the wagons creaking ominously where the heat had warped wood and metal and brought the grease dripping from the joints to fall into the sand beneath them. Soon, if they were not able to stop and regrease the wheels and axles, they would find themselves running in dry joints and half an hour of that would be enough to wreck a wagon almost beyond repair.

They were half a mile further on when they heard the steady abrasion of horses in the distance. Leaning sideways, Kirby peered around the flapping canvas of the wagon. Through the dust wake, he was able to make out the solitary rider spurring his way towards them, and behind him, perhaps two miles distant, a larger dust cloud which betokened a big bunch of men. He heard the gunfire die into a silence made more hollow by the din that had preceded it. By now, the outriders had all come in except for Charlie Rodgers. This would be him, making it back as fast as he could push his tired mount, Kirby thought. Then, as the man drew nearer he noticed the way he was slumped sideways in the saddle, the manner in which he seemed to be having some difficulty in remaining upright; and he knew at once that the other had been hurt.

Elston, too, had seen Rodgers' plight. Spurring his horse, he rode out to meet him, caught him as he swayed and would have fallen from the saddle. Holding him upright with one hand, keeping his own mount close to the other's, he guided him towards the wagon train. Two men jumped down from one of the wagons, helped Rodgers down and carried him on to the tongue of a wagon.

Bending over the other, Elston said quietly: 'What happened, Charlie?'

'Quentin and his men. About thirty of 'em. Just behind me on the trail. I spotted 'em half an hour ago.'

'All right. Just lie still and we'll get that wound seen to.' Gently, he opened the other's shirt, stared down at the wound in the other's chest where the bullet had penetrated all the way through. He knew with a sickening sense of hopelessness that the other's lung had certainly been punctured, that there was nothing they could do and it was only a matter of minutes before he died.

Hastily, he scanned the ground ahead of them. There was a range of low ridges less than half a mile away. If they could get the wagons there, into the narrow pass which lay between the rolling folds of ground, they might be able to take up a defensive position where there was a chance of holding out. Here, in the open, it would be easy for Quentin and his outfit to surround them and pin them down.

'Get the wagons moving,' he yelled at the top of his voice. He pointed to the rocks. 'Into that canyon yonder. It's our only chance.'

Shouting, slashing, cajoling, cursing, the men got the oxen moving, lumbering through the treacherous dust towards the rocks. Leaping back into the saddle, Elston urged his own mount into a dispirited run, sorry for the horse as he rammed rowels into its flesh. Behind them, a ragged burst of shots broke the lull.

Careening over the plain, the wagons converged on the entrance to the canyon. The first plunged in, continued on for a couple of hundred yards before the man in the driver's seat pulled back on the reins, his legs braced against the front of the wagon. Sliding almost on to their haunches, the oxen came to a slithering halt. The rest of the wagons cut in behind them. Almost before they had stopped, the men had dropped to the ground, grabbing at their Winchesters and Springfields, racing for the rocks, throwing themselves flat on their bellies and peering off into the cloud of dust they had lifted in their flight, waiting for the first targets to appear before they opened fire.

Lying there, watchful and alert, Kirby felt his shoulders tense, told himself angrily to relax. A shoulder can't stop a .45 slug, so there was little point in getting so tensed up. But he could still feel the tightness working its way through him, coiling the muscles of his chest and stomach, knotting them painfully. His vision was blurred and for seconds at a time he seemed to be seeing everything double.

Two shots came from the rocks on the other side of the canyon. The dust was settling now and he was just able to make out the bunch of men reining to a halt less than two hundred yards from the mouth of the canyon. He snapped a quick shot at one man, saw him drop from the saddle, but it wasn't possible for him to tell from the way the other fell, whether his bullet had found its mark or not.

He raised the Winchester again, propped it in a vee in the rocks, and squinted along the barrel, sighting on the spot where he had seen two of the other men go down. He waited, drawing air slowly into his lungs, acutely aware that sweat from his forehead was dripping into his eyebrows and would soon be running into his eyes, half blinding him. Seconds passed.

There!

The figure, doubled over to present a more difficult target, came running across his line of vision. The split second that he saw it, he fired. Too late. The man was out of sight behind the milling horses. He studied the terrain thoughtfully. They were slightly higher than the Connaught outfit and the others were caught in the more open ground with very little cover. A slug broke rock less than a foot above his head and he pulled himself down sharply, cursing his inattention that had almost cost him his life. Crawling along behind the cover of the rocks, he paused then raised his head slowly until he was looking down on the Connaught outfit's position from another angle. Now he could just make out the legs and lower half of the body of one of the men lying flat on his belly behind the horses. Grinning a little to himself, Kirby lifted the Winchester, sighted it carefully and pulled the trigger. He saw the man's body jerk, saw the legs drum the ground for a few seconds and then lie still.

More gunfire had broken out all along the line of rocks, pouring a hail of lead into Quentin's positions. Sooner or later, the other was going to have to make a move, thought Kirby. He could not afford to stay out there in the open much longer or he ran the risk of losing all of his men without inflicting any damage at all on the wagon train and its crew. All of this went through Kirby's mind as he watched the scene below him. He deliberated the position, tried to put himself into Quentin's mind, tried to figure out what he would do in the other's place.

As far as he could see, there was only one course open to the other. He would have to get his men under cover and that meant moving across the open ground and into the rocks on the edge of the canyon. Sooner or later, they are going to do that, he figured. Even as the thought flashed through his mind, a heavy volley of gunfire broke out from the Connaught outfit. Instinctively, he pulled his head down as lead smacked and whined among the rocks on all sides of him.

Before the firing had slackened, he raised himself stiffly, grabbed for his Colt, knowing the Winchester was far too unwieldy for a job like this. The roar of the three shots came so close together it sounded like a single explosion. One man, racing for the rocks skidded as his legs stiffened, he reeled, straightened, took two halting steps forward and then sagged drunkenly to the dust, falling backwards and lying still. Another Connaught rider fell but the rest of them gained the sanctuary of the rocks at the foot of the canyon walls.

Kirby shifted to the end of the narrow ledge on which he was crouched, glanced down. An inquisitive head poked itself up from the boulders and his Colt spat viciously. A man yelled harshly and the head disappeared.

Kirby returned his attention to the spot where the other men had gone down. There was a brief lull in the firing and a few seconds later, a harsh voice that he recognised as Elmore's called: 'You up there, Elston?'

A few feet from Kirby, Matt Elston looked

up at the unexpected sound of his name. He could not see Bat and he lay quite still in the blistering heat of the sun, his carbine tight against his cheek and did not answer.

'Elston!'

He waited tensely. Every muscle in him was so tight that he began to ache; and the big muscles along his legs and thighs were cramped. But his mind was very clear and very sharp. He heard every sound from down below as if it were strangely magnified in importance. A man shifted his position somewhere out of sight and a wounded man was moaning monotonously near the cluster of horses. He had followed the movements of Quentin's men, had seen them dart across the open space the instant the heavy volley of gunfire had ceased and he knew that although a handful of them had been killed or wounded, most of them were still alive and under cover. He bit his lower lip indecisively. Down there, it would be relatively easy for those *hombres* to scatter and move around to encircle the wagons. He wondered where Earl Quentin was; whether he had ridden out with his men or stayed back in Yuma to keep his eye on things there. More shots erupted from the men on his right, but for the most part, he reckoned they were simply shooting at shadows. The Connaught men were staying well under cover now.

Earl Quentin arrived at the scene half an hour later. The racket of gunfire was still going on. The sound had carried far over the desert, the echoes of the shots reverberating through the mouth of the canyon. At the first hint of sound, both men had reined abruptly. Then Quentin drew his lips back over his teeth and said, grinning: 'That's quite a ways off, up near those hills, I reckon. Bat must've come on the wagon train yonder and pinned em down.'

The man with him scanned the ground ahead through narrowed, speculative eyes. He did not speak for several moments, then muttered grimly: 'Sounds like quite a battle. Hear those rifles blastin'. Could be that the Overland crew were ready for 'em, but it's hard to be sure with so many echoes bouncing about.' He turned his head, looked along the range of hills. 'I figure it might be wise if we was to approach from the south, at least until we've discovered who's pinned down who.'

Quentin's eyes narrowed as he pondered that. He had not even given a thought to the possibility that the Overland outfit could have turned the tables on Bat and the rest of the boys, but now that the other had mentioned it, he grudgingly had to admit to himself that there was just the chance it had happened that way. The Overland crew would have been on the look out for trouble, would almost certainly have had outriders out on the flanks and to cover their rear, to give warning of any impending attack.

He gave a brief nod of his head, pulled his hat brim well down over his eyes, wiped the sweat from his face with his bandana and then urged his tired mount forward, away from the trail, striking well to the south, zig-zagging across the treacherously shifting sand. This was going to be damnably hard on their horses, he knew. Their hooves sank deeply into the sand and they could not make good time for fear of being thrown.

Twenty minutes of torture passed as they angled towards the rocky slope. The roar of gunfire was deafening now, but once they had swung around the southern edge of the hills, it became muffled. Getting down from his horse, he motioned to the other to do likewise, leading his own mount forward. Jagged rocks scraped their flesh and sent them stumbling. The trail they had found played out through gravel and chunks of rock until they reached a spot where the horses had to be left behind, the trail not wide enough for them to squeeze through.

Quentin pointed to a path, twisted and choked with tangled brush and boulders that snaked away and upward to the edge of the pinkish-red mesa that had been deeply eroded by the winds. The trail was little more than a game track, though what sort of game ever came as far out into the desert as this, Quentin could not imagine. Clinging to precarious handholds, shinned over rough boulders and crumbling rock outcrops, making full use of the grotesque fissures, they climbed to the top, threw themselves down among the rocks.

A few moments later, Quentin edged forward an inch at a time, glanced down and saw the wagon train almost immediately beneath him. It seemed deserted, except for the body of one man lying just inside the second wagon in the line. Squinting down, he could just make out the legs and boots of the other, thrust out from the shade inside, reckoned him to be either dead or wounded and at once dismissed the man's presence there from his calculations. There wasn't any sign of the rest of the outfit and he let his narrowed-down gaze wander over the rocky gulches to either side of the canyon, caught the occasional muzzle flash and puff of rifle smoke that told him where most of them were.

His own men he noticed, were at the very eastern edge of the narrow, high-sided canyon. From there, they could pin down the wagon train, but it would be a long job to smoke every last one of the defenders out of their positions.

He felt a touch on his arm, looked down into the cold, pale face of the gunfighter.

'There's their water supply,' hissed the other, pointing to the wagon that lay directly beneath them. 'If they was to lose all of that, you could just up and leave 'em. They'd never make it anywhere.'

He raised his Winchester as he spoke, sighting it on the wooden barrels secured around the wagon, finger tight on the trigger, taking up the slack slowly.

Quentin nodded. 'That's an idea,' he agreed. He hauled his own rifle forward. From that distance, it was impossible to miss. The crash of their rifles was lost in the general racket which boomed along the canyon. Carefully, feeling a kind of vicious satisfaction, he pumped bullet after bullet into the barrels, saw the water spurt from them in glistening streams, splashing on to the sand beneath, where it pooled briefly and was then gone, sucked up avidly by the parched earth.

With daylight, Wayne and the two Overland riders followed the trail more cautiously. There was no need to watch the sides of the trail now, for trouble. The first pale grey streaks of dawn had been colouring the eastern horizon when they had spotted the bunch of Connaught men in the distance. Wayne had felt a sudden twinge of doubt when he had noticed that there were two men travelling some distance behind the main body of riders but the reason for this had become crystal clear when they had heard the first break of gunfire to the west and had seen the two figures pause in deep conversation and then light out to the south. Quentin and the gunslinger who had ridden into town, Wayne had guessed, not wanting to risk their necks in an unexpected brush with the wagon train. Evidently they had decided to follow at a safe distance biding their time until they saw how things were going.

'Do we follow Quentin and that gun-slinger, or cut over yonder and try to take the main bunch from the rear?' asked Slim. He wiped his face with the back of his hand, stared down at the smear of dust on it.

Wayne looked across the half mile or more of open ground which lay between them and the hills. 'They could spot us before we got there,' he said musingly, 'though I figure they'll have their work cut out keepin' their heads down.' He looked round at the other two but their faces were devoid of any expression. They were clearly leaving it up to him to make the decision. Maybe he should have moved more quickly during the night, come up on Quentin and that gun-hawk before they knew there was anyone trailing them. Now there was not time to sit thinking about what he ought to have done, though as he lifted himself a little in the saddle, he could still make out the two figures approaching the southern rim of the hills, obviously intent on working their way around the party trapped in the canyon.

'We'd better split up,' he said finally. 'I'll trail Quentin and that other *hombre*. You two cut over the desert behind the main bunch. Watch your step when you get to the foothills. There's a chance you might run foul of our own fire.'

Yarrow nodded, answering: 'That's the

best way, I guess.'

Wayne waited as the others rode off, then gigged his own mount off the trail. The sign made by Quentin and his companion was clearly visible in the middle-down sun, but further on, as the sand gave way to more rocky ground, the hoofmarks were less apparent. The two men had vanished from sight now among the rocks, but there seemed very few places where they would be able to climb up to the ledges from this direction and although there were long stretches where he had no sign to follow, he chose one particular path to the hills simply because it seemed more direct than any of the others, and the one which the two men were most likely to have followed.

Fifteen minutes later, he entered the narrowness of the rocky defile, straining eyes and ears for any sign of trouble. Two shots came from somewhere high up, the sound beating back down the slope to him, sharp and clear. He noticed that the regular beat of gunfire from the main force was muffled by the looming bulk of the rocks, knew that either Quentin or the gunman had fired and reckoned they were crouched down among the boulders almost directly above him. Dropping from the saddle, he led the horse forward and two minutes later, rounding a sharp bend in the defile, he came upon the other two horses, standing patiently hipshot in a small clearing. Beyond them, he noticed where the trail led up to the higher levels.

Leaving his own mount there, he pulled the Colt from its holster and started up the trail, clawing his way over some of the roughest terrain he had ever encountered. More shots came from above him and then silence. Sweating profusely, he pulled himself up, pausing whenever loose rocks and stones bounced down the slope from beneath his feet. The pathway in places sloped so steeply upwards that there were piles of loose rubble which had obviously cascaded down from above and it was doubly difficult to move here without making any sound. Towards the end, he was forced to thrust the Colt back into its holster and use both hands to haul himself up, fingers raw and bleeding as he was forced to hang on to narrow, razor-edged ledges and fissures to gain a handhold. The cliff was rock and a thin covering of earth, with no true vegetation beyond a few clumps of brown, withered grass. Once, near the top, his boots slipped in the shale and he swung outward into space and downward, dropping until his chest scraped painfully against the rim of the narrow ledge just above him. With an effort, he got one elbow hooked over the rocks and hung on grimly, all of the air forced out of his lungs, a moment's sharp pain in his chest. Desperately, he tried to anchor himself against the rock face. Sweat dripped continually into his eyes, mingling with the dust, blinding him. Working his feet, he kicked at the rock wall below him, moved them slowly up and down struggling to find a toehold by which he could steady himself. He could feel the strength draining from his body, leaving him limp. Then, when it seemed he could not possibly hold on for another moment, his right toe jammed into a narrow crevice in the rock. It was no more than three inches across, but it was enough. He hung there for a long moment drawing air down into his lungs, waiting until his vision cleared and the painful throbbing in his head eased a little. Then he lifted himself gently, elbows taking the strain from his leg, knowing that the foothold was very insecure and a wrong move could send him crashing down into the rocks below. Gathering his strength, he remained poised there for five seconds, then lunged forward and upward, catching his chest on the ledge. Once more, all of the wind was knocked from him, but he was more than half way over and presently he found the strength to twist himself to one side, getting his right knee on to the ledge and levering himself up. He rolled forward, lay there panting harshly. The harsh glare of the sunlight in his eyes made the throbbing behind his forehead grow in intensity until it was as if someone were pounding with a hammer inside his skull.

Drawing in a deep shuddering breath, he scrambled to his feet, kneeling there as he listened intently for any sound of movement above him. The silence continued and he guessed that he had not been heard.

He crawled along behind the cover of the rocks. Ten feet along the ledge and the ground levelled off. Now, he moved more cautiously, heard the scrape of a boot on stone and hesitated, drawing the Colt as he risked a quick look around the side of a tall boulder.

There was no sign of anyone there. It was possible that Quentin had moved on after firing those shots, that he and the other had worked their way down the slope towards the wagons, probably hoping to take the defenders by surprise from the rear. But Wayne was in no mood to take chances now. He stole along the narrow ledge, keeping his head down, silent and watchful as a stalking cougar.

In a few moments, he saw the man spreadeagled on the flat rocks less than ten feet away in the shade of a stunted bush that seemed to grow out of the very rock. The other lay quite still, his cheek pressed against the stock of his rifle. It was Earl Quentin. Beyond him, in the floor of the canyon, Wayne could see the wagons, drawn up in a line. There was a faint movement near one of the wagons and he narrowed his eyes as he recognised the form of the gunfighter who had been with Quentin. The other was edging towards the lead wagon, gun in hand.

Was the other hoping to get inside and drive it away before Elston and the others knew he was there? Or could there be some other reason for his actions? Then, at once, Wayne knew. Outwardly that wagon was no different from any of the others. But no doubt when he had moved into the Overland yard in his attempt to set the train on fire, Bat Elmore had discovered what it contained and had passed the word on to

Quentin. Whereas the rest of the wagons contained food and the usual stores, the lead wagon carried all of the guns, ammunition and dynamite needed by the Army.

It was too late to stop the other now. The man had dropped out of sight behind the wagon, crawling on his hands and knees around the far side. Wayne knew there was only one chance now.

Gliding forward among the rocks, he moved up close behind Earl Quentin, the other totally oblivious of his presence. Levelling the Colt on the man's back, he said harshly, 'Let go that rifle and get on your feet, Quentin, or I'm likely to plug you right off.'

He saw the other stiffen abruptly. For a split second the man's fingers tightened convulsively on the stock of the Winchester, then he forced them to relax, thrust the gun away from him as if it were a dangerous snake, and lay still, not turning his head.

'I said get on your feet, Quentin!' Wayne snapped. He suited his words by stepping right up to the other and ramming the barrel of the Colt into his back.

This time, Quentin obeyed without hesitation. He said hoarsely: 'You're too late, Everett. The Morenci Kid is down there right now. Any second and he'll have his hands on that explosive in the wagon. Then you're all finished.'

Wayne shook his head. He deliberately forced evenness into his voice. 'You don't get it, Quentin. I'm giving you ten seconds to call off your men – and that includes your gunman yonder, or I'll smash your spine with a bullet.'

He saw sweat start out afresh on the other's darkly handsome features. The other licked his lips as Wayne began to count, slowly and deliberately.

'Five, six, seven...'

Quentin's lips twitched and there was a tiny muscle throbbing uncontrollably high in his cheek. He shifted his stance a little, grunted with pain as Wayne thrust the Colt harder into the small of his back. 'Do you reckon that beatin' Mary Vender is worth losin' your life, Quentin?' he hissed thinly.

'You're bluffin',' said the other, his tone ragged. 'You know that–'

'Eight, nine...' went on Wayne remorselessly. The hammer of the gun clicked loudly as he levered it back with his thumb.

Quentin's face blanched. His lips were twisted into a harsh grimace. Then he blurted out, 'All right, damn you!' Raising his voice to a shout, he yelled: 'Cease firin', men. This is Earl Quentin! Stop shootin'.'

His high-pitched cry echoed down into the canyon. The thunder of gunfire ceased slowly, with only an occasional sporadic shot being fired. Out of the corner of his eye, Wayne watched the lead wagon below him. He said harshly: 'Get that gunslinger of yours out into the open where I can see him, tell him to throw down his guns.'

'Get away from that wagon, Kid.' There was a note of terror in the other's voice now. 'Do as I say. Everett has got the drop on me.'

There was a pause, then slowly, the short figure of the gunman came into sight from around the back of the wagon. Wayne let his breath go in a soundless sigh of relief. There had been a dangerous moment then when it had seemed that the gunman did not intend to obey Quentin's order, when his vicious nature might have taken over and he would have gone through with his plan of blowing up that wagon full of dynamite, possibly relying on getting away in the resulting confusion.

'Drop your gunbelts, all of you,' Quentin yelled.

One by one, the Connaught outfit came

out of their holes, shucking their gunbelts. Wayne watched with satisfaction. Thrusting Quentin in front of him, he made the other move down the winding track which led down to the floor of the canyon. The Connaught outfit stood in sullen groups as Matt Elston and the others moved out of the rocks.

Matt grinned at Wayne. 'I guess we finally got this bunch right where we want 'em,' he said. 'What do you reckon we should do with 'em?'

Wayne motioned to the Connaught men. 'Saddle up and ride on out of here,' he said thinly. 'If you want my advice, forget about Quentin. He's finished. Ride on over the hill and keep ridin'. The next time we'll gun you down.'

'You reckon that's wise?' queried Elston. 'Turnin' them loose like this.'

'Without Quentin, they're nothin' but gun trash,' Wayne told him. 'They work for any man who pays them wages and gives them shelter from the law. But once they get neither, they owe him no more allegiance. I've met up with their sort before. They won't trouble us none now.'

'Hope you know what you're doin',' grunted the other. He did not seem as sure

193

about it as Wayne was.

'Stands to reason we can't take 'em with us, either to the nearest Army outpost or back to Yuma. We don't have the men to keep an eye on all of them.'

He watched keenly as the men moved back to their horses, swung up into the saddle, turned their mounts about and headed out across the desert, kicking up a cloud of dust behind them.

Elston turned to face Quentin and the Kid. He jerked a thumb at them. 'What do we do with these two?'

Wayne's lips twisted into a sardonic grin. 'I'm takin' these two men back to Yuma. They'll stand trial there. This is the end of the trail for you, Quentin.' His glance flicked to the sallow-faced man standing beside the other. 'And for the Morenci Kid.' There was something about his smile that forced the gunman to shift his gaze.

Yarrow came forward, leathering his Colt. He paused as he saw the man standing next to Quentin, then said thinly, in a curiously wondering tone. 'That *hombre* ain't the Morenci Kid.'

'He ain't?' said Elston.

'Too right he's not. I've met up with this coyote before. He's a two-bit killer from Los

Lobos goin' by the name of Kerrick. Wanted for murder in half a dozen towns.'

Wayne nodded. 'That's what I figured,' he rapped. He turned his glance on Earl Quentin. 'You had to have somebody you could use to keep the town under your thumb and when the Morenci Kid never showed up like you'd expected, you had to do somethin' fast, otherwise you saw your chances slippin' away. So you sent word through to Los Lobos for this coyote. Nobody in Yuma had seen the Morenci Kid so you reckoned you'd be safe enough, at least until you'd done all you'd set out to do.'

Quentin's lips twisted into a snarl. 'I can still do that, Everett. The only way you can stop me is to shoot Kerrick and me down right here, murder us in cold blood. Because you've still got to get us to Yuma and that's more than three days' ride from here, using tired horses. Three days across that desert and without water.' His grin widened as he noticed the look on the faces of the listening men. 'That's right.' An odd edge of tension heightened the pitch of his voice. 'And the same goes for the rest of you. You made a mistake lettin' the rest of the boys go without takin' what water they had. Have a look behind you at the water barrels. Not a drop left. And there ain't a waterhole within thirty miles that hasn't been dried up months ago.'

7

HELL TRAIL

Everett waited patiently in the scalding heat of the late afternoon, watched as the teamsters climbed on to the wagons, cracked the long, rawhide whips over the backs of the oxen. Slowly, the wheels turned as they were dragged free of the dust which sloughed off the turning spokes like water. Moving through the canyon, they headed out to the west. It would be a hard trail for those men with scarcely any water left to see them through the burning hell of the desert that lay ahead of them, but here they had been at the point of no return as far as the wagon train was concerned. It was, if anything, slightly less distance to the Army outpost than it was back to Yuma. Either way a man would go through hell before he reached safety.

As the last of the wagons creaked out of the canyon, he allowed his attention to turn to the predicament of Yarrow and himself. Half a canteen each, and two prisoners who would be waiting every moment for the next two days and three nights, hoping to catch them off guard. It had been a hard, hot ride out from Yuma. Going back would be a thousand times more difficult and dangerous.

The scalding heat thrown up from the sand burned through the soles of his boots. Sweat had soaked into his shirt and it was sticking to his back, chafing the flesh raw with every movement he made.

Turning to Quentin, he said sharply, 'All right, mount up. And remember, the first move either of you make that I don't like, and it will be your last.'

Quentin climbed sullenly into the saddle. Kerrick swung up, stared with empty, dark eyes down at Everett. 'You won't be able to watch us for every single minute of the way, Everett,' he said bleakly, but with a certain malicious enjoyment. 'Not even if you take it in turns to sleep. You've both ridden the past two nights with very little sleep, if you had any at all. And in this heat, with only enough water to last you for a day, you'll both be so exhausted that you won't be able to keep your eyes open.' His teeth showed in an animal-like grin. 'The first time, Everett – and you're finished. Just chew on that for a while.'

'Get moving,' was all that Everett said. He swung into the saddle, waited until Yarrow had done likewise, then prodded his mount forward. The blazing disc of the sun lay behind them now, dropping slowly from its zenith to the western horizon, throwing their black shadows in front of them along the sand.

He could hear the faint splash of the water in the canteen that hung by his side and the sound seemed to grow in his ears like the swell of the sea washing on to rocks. With a tremendous effort, he tried to shut his mind to it, knowing that he could not afford to dwell on their difficulties.

Quentin and Kerrick sat low in their saddles, peering straight ahead of them, their faces empty masks through which only their eyes showed alive and speculative. The desert sun beat down on the backs of their necks. Out in the distance more dust devils lifted in whorls that spun crazily for several seconds before settling down and vanishing from sight as if they had never existed. As he rode, Wayne studied the face of the desert, examining it section by section. There was a little nagging thought at the back of his mind, which continually intruded on his consciousness, worrying him more than he cared to admit, even to himself.

He could see no sign of Quentin's men, although their tracks were clearly visible at intervals. There was just the chance that they had only withdrawn to what they considered to be a safe distance, that they may have guessed at his intentions as far as Quentin was concerned, reckoning on him taking the other back to Yuma to stand trial. If that was so, they could easily be lying in wait for them somewhere among the brush where the two stretches of desert were divided by the range of hills through which he and the others had ridden early the previous night. If this were indeed so, then Bat Elmore would find it an ideal spot to stage an ambush.

Almost as if he had divined Wayne's thoughts, Quentin said hoarsely: 'You gettin' a mite worried, Everett? Maybe figurin' that it was a mistake bringin' us this way?'

Wayne said nothing, knowing that the other was deliberately trying to provoke him.

The Connaught boss went on relentlessly: 'Those men of mine won't have ridden as far as you reckon. They'll be watchin' the trail back to Yuma, waitin' for us to show up. Then where will you be. You can't hope to fight them off. And even if you kill me, they'll get you. Why don't you act sensibly? Turn Kerrick and me loose here, we'll make it to the border and there's nothin' more for you to worry about.'

'You're just wastin' your breath, Quentin,' Wayne said tightly.

'Am I? You're no lawman. What's your position here? You ride into town and start actin' like a do-gooder for no reason at all.' He paused, then looked back at Wayne, a look of realisation on his face. 'Unless you've fallen in love with Mary Vender. Sure, that could be it. Why didn't I think of that before?' His grin was mocking. 'You'll never make out there. She's too damned busy runnin' that broken-down freighting company to worry about a saddle-loose drifter like you. I know her. If she ever marries at all, it'll be to some banker or the like with enough money to keep her in style. Guess it was havin' schoolin' back East that did this for her. Still, I reckon that–'

Angrily, Everett gigged his mount over to the other's, drew back his hand and slashed the other across the face with the flat of his palm. 'Shut up, Quentin,' he rasped tautly. 'I won't warn you again.'

'The hell you won't,' said the other. An

angry red mark showed on his face. 'You'd like to pull your gun and shoot me down right now, wouldn't you? All because you know I'm speakin' the truth and that is one thing you can't take.'

Wayne drew back his hand again, fingers knotted into a clenched fist. Then he lowered his arm as Yarrow said: 'Relax, Wayne. He's only tryin' to get you riled.'

For a long moment, Wayne stared into Quentin's grinning face, then forced his anger down with an effort. He recognised that what Yarrow said was the truth. Quentin was determined to wear him down, to get his nerves all on edge. Swallowing thickly, he moved his mount away from the other's, taking up his original position a little to the rear of the two men.

The fine ashy dust that rose up under the feet of the horses hung like a moving cloud about them, getting into their mouths and nostrils, working its way beneath their eyelids. Wayne rode bent over in the saddle to minimise the effect of the glare and the heat. In the desert, time seemed to melt and run together under the molten sun and the long minutes dragged themselves into still longer hours. Wayne allowed no rest stops, knowing this would only increase the chances of Quentin putting any plan he might be thinking up, into operation. So long as the two men were in the saddle and in front of him, there was little they could do. But dismounted, it would be difficult to keep an eye on both of them unless they were tied up.

With the gradual decline of the sun at their backs, a wind came up. At first it was the merest breath of air blowing into their faces but over the torturous minutes, its strength rapidly grew. It was not cool but stingingly hot and it lifted the sand in clouds, the face of the desert shifting liquidly like a great yellow sea all around them. Burning gusts of sand became a swarming darkness composed of millions of irritating particles that blotted out the glaring blue-white of the late afternoon heaven, turning it to a dull, angry grey and behind them, the sun was a swollen bloated disc which glared at them evilly like a crimson eye staring down at them pitilessly from the sky.

Rising in pitch, the wind shrieked around them, buffeting them from all sides as it seemed to switch direction from one second to the next. The horses walked forward now with a shuffling gait, heads lowered, struggling to turn their backs on it, fighting against the pull on the reins as the men fought to keep them moving east.

Every breath they tried to take went down like fire, stabbing at their lungs, their chest muscles painful with the effort of breathing. Over their heads, great sheets of yellow seared against the heavens. All sound was drowned, swamped utterly by the noise of the wind as the sandstorm closed about them.

Wayne had been through one of these great storms before, had never wanted to be caught in another. They had been known to last for days, although this usually only happened when the northers began to blow. With an east wind, they usually died down at the end of an hour or so; but it would be an hour plucked from the depths of a nightmare.

Ten minutes later, they were forced to dismount, crouched down in the dust behind the horses, their bandanas over the lower halves of their faces in an attempt to filter out the dust. Fury roared around them. Wayne stared down dully at the desert floor beneath him, his mind numbed, his brain curiously empty. The millions of individual grains that went to make up the ground beneath him flowed and eddied like smoke beneath his fingers. Lifting his head, he glanced through slitted eyes to where Quentin and Kerrick knelt behind their mounts. At the moment, neither man seemed to have any thoughts of trying to make a break for it. Not that they would get far in this, he pondered numbly. Indeed, it was extremely doubtful if they would be able to make the horses move even if they did attempt to get up into the saddle.

It was a weird sight beneath the terrible sky, the swirling clouds moving all around them, the world closing in on them in a shrieking, howling maelstrom as the wind blew at their clothing. Even with the horse sheltering him, his mouth and eyes were full of sand. He tried to spit it out, but his throat and lips were so cracked and dry that it was impossible. Tired, racked by a feeling of sickness, he closed his eyes and mouth, but it was out of the question to close his ears to the dreadful noise, or his mind to the insensate fury of the dust storm.

How long the storm lasted it was difficult to estimate. It seemed to sustain its high pitch of fury for an interminable time. But gradually, almost imperceptibly at first, there seemed to be some lessening to the force of the wind. At first, he could scarcely believe that it was happening, thought it was merely his imagination, did not want to believe it for fear that it was not true. But as the long, drawn-out minutes passed, the realisation came to him that the wind was abating, the fury of the storm was slackening. The sky lightened above their heads and slowly, it was possible to make out details of the territory. He wiped the caked dust from his face, clawed it out of his eyes and tried to spit it from his mouth once more as he straightened up, then staggered to his feet, swaying as the last gusts of wind caught at him, taking him completely by surprise.

A few moments later, the other three men rose to their feet and peered about them. Dribbling a little water into his mouth, he swilled it around his teeth, then swallowed, feeling a little better.

'Let's move out,' he croaked hoarsely. Even the effort of speaking, hurt his throat and chest. 'The storm's over and we've got some distance to cover before nightfall.'

Quentin grunted. He muttered: 'You figurin' on ridin' clear through the night, Everett?'

'That's right. You got any objections?'

'Nope. I reckon Kerrick and me can just

doze in the saddle. We'll still be pretty fresh by mornin' whereas the two of you will be dead beat unless you try to take it in turn to drop off.'

'We can always do that,' said Yarrow tensely. He jerked a savage look at the Connaught boss. 'On the other hand, when it's my turn to keep watch, I might just get the idea we'd be better off savin' the citizens of Yuma all the cost and trouble of a trial and I'll plug both of you.' The way he said it left little doubt in Quentin's mind that he meant every word. Even Everett gave the other a worried look. There was the chance that Yarrow's nerve and self-control might snap before they even got within sight of Yuma and the man would no longer be responsible for his actions.

With the retreat of the storm to the west, the sky cleared swiftly and the air became cooler and cleaner. Wayne sat weakly in the saddle, allowing the horse to pick its own gait. The sun was close to the horizon now and their shadows were long before them. All around, the desert seemed to have been wiped clean, apart from the short length of hoofmarks that lay immediately in their wake. Smoothed out by the wind, the sand lay flat and featureless as far as the eye could see. At least, that was how it appeared for a while.

When Wayne saw the buzzards first, wheeling like tattered strips of black cloth against the darkening purple of the eastern sky, he had to stare at them for several moments before he was certain they were not spots conjured up by his sand-seared vision.

'Buzzards,' said Yarrow a moment later. 'You figure there might be water up ahead?'

'Not this stop,' Wayne said wearily. 'Could be somethin' else though.'

Five minutes later, they saw the two dark specks on the sand. They lay in a shallow gully which explained why they had not been able to pick them out earlier.

'There they are,' said Yarrow dully. 'Reckon you were right, Wayne.'

They rode on and as they neared the two dark mounds that lay unmoving in the yellow dust, a flock of the hideous creatures lifted into the air, wings flapping noisily as they climbed up with angry cries. Wayne pushed his vision through the reddish haze that hovered in front of his eyes, felt a little revolted at what he saw. Reining up their mounts, the four men leaned forward in their saddles, staring down at the two bodies which lay there, legs and arms twisted into unnatural positions, heads lolling on one side, eyes ugly, faces almost unrecognisable.

Sharply, Wayne said: 'You know these men, Quentin?'

The other ran the tip of his tongue over his lips. Hesitantly, he said: 'I'm not sure. They don't look like–'

'Get down and take a closer look. They could be a couple of your men. If they were badly wounded durin' the gunfight back there, then I reckon the rest of the boys wouldn't want to have to drag 'em along, slowin' their pace and makin' it more risky in the desert. They'd just leave 'em behind for the vultures.'

Still Quentin hesitated, then as Wayne laid his glance on him, he slipped from the saddle, and walked forward, every step reluctant. Bending, he stooped over the nearer man, turned him over. Wayne saw the Connaught boss's shoulders heave a little as nausea swept over him. Then, almost without warning, Quentin's right hand moved towards the gunbelt that the dead man wore. Had he not been expecting a move such as this, Wayne would have been taken completely by surprise.

Before Quentin could swing round

however and level the gun in his hand, the Colt in Wayne's hand spoke sharply and a bullet ploughed into the sand within an inch of Quentin's body.

'Drop it! If you don't, it's the last move you'll ever make.' As if the gun was red-hot, Quentin dropped it into the dirt beside him, eased himself slowly to his feet.

'That's better. You don't know how close you were to lookin' the man with the scythe in the face. Now back on your horse.'

He waited until the other had complied with the order, then said softly, very softly: 'You still haven't answered my first question, Quentin. Do you know either of those two men?'

'Yes. They're Vickers and Holmes. Two of my boys. They'd both been shot.'

'That's just how I'd figured it.' Wayne thrust the gun back into leather, kicked spurs against the stallion's flanks. As they moved away, the vultures overhead began their slow descending spirals, moving down towards the two still mounds.

In the cold night air, the sweat on Wayne's body congealed and he felt himself freezingly cold in the saddle. Both Quentin and Kerrick were dozing as they rode, occasionally jerking back to sudden awareness as their mounts stumbled on the rough ground. Swaying, Wayne fought against the tiredness which threatened to overwhelm him. Weariness was a fine drawn-out agony in every nerve and fibre of his body, limbs and brain crying out for sleep. The heat of the day, drawing the moisture from him out of every pore, had dehydrated him to the extent where it was impossible to think straight. Strange thoughts and images crowded into his mind, evoking memories of days he had thought were long since forgotten. The warm grasslands he had known as a boy, with the great herds of cattle grazing on them, a sea of sleek brown backs and tossing horns which stretched almost as far as the eye could see. The vast apple orchards with the fruit hanging red and golden on the trees and the scent of blossom in the air on a crisp May morning with the frost and dew glittering brilliantly on the grass and branches.

Angrily, he forced his wandering mind back to the present, recognising the danger signals. His brain had almost sunk deeply into the black abyss of unconsciousness and as he jerked his head upright, looked about him, he saw Quentin's tall shape limmed against the night sky, edging his mount a little closer to his. Another few moments and the other would have reached out with his right hand and snatched his Colt from its holster.

In a low, thin tone, he said: 'Get back where I can see you properly, Quentin. Another move like that and I'll be the one to shoot you out of the saddle.'

Quentin uttered a harsh laugh, oddly mocking in its intensity, pulled a little on the reins, moving his horse back a few feet.

'It'll come soon, Everett,' he said sarcastically. 'You can't hold out much longer without sleep. The heat and the storm have taken more out of you than you dare to admit. There are more than seven hours of the night to get through yet and another fourteen hours of scorching hell tomorrow and we still won't have come within sight of Yuma. And even if you do succeed in gettin' back to town – what then? Hand us over to the sheriff? He won't take the word of a trail drifter against mine.'

'He'll take it, or I'll toss him in jail along with you,' said Wayne savagely. 'Now just keep your eyes on the trail in front of you. If you start fidgeting again, I may get it into my head you're itchin' to try somethin' and

I'll shoot first and ask any questions afterwards.'

'You ain't the type to shoot a man in the back without givin' him a chance. I know your kind. You think you're big and so you live by a code all your own. You'd sooner run the risk of being shot in an even draw than kill a man who isn't carryin' a gun. That's what will be the finish of you very soon. Because I know exactly what I want and I won't let anythin' stand in the way of gettin' it. I'm a different breed of man to you. I kill and murder so long as it means I get my own way.'

'Shut up and save your breath,' Wayne said harshly. There was a set, grim mask to his face and a kind of silent fury deep inside him. There had been a ring of truth to what the other had said which had made a deep impression on him in spite of himself. Maybe things would be better if he was to kill both of these men now. Had the positions been reversed, Quentin would have done that, without giving it a second thought.

Three hours before daybreak, he was forced to call a halt. The horses were faltering at almost every step. They had been denied water and the strain had taken its toll on them. Ground reining the horses, they sat in two small groups on the cold sand. Lying on his side, Wayne watched the two men while Yarrow slept. His head pillowed on his hat, his snoring a hard, grunting sound in the deep stillness that lay over the desert. It was bitterly cold. Overhead, the stars held a brilliant, diamond-like hardness, so close he felt he had only to lift his little finger to be able to touch them. To keep himself awake and alert, he let his gaze wander occasionally over the great inverted arch of the heavens, picking out the constellations that marched in ordered glory from horizon to horizon.

Quentin sat silent and unmoving a few yards away, his gaze fixed on Wayne's face. There was something inscrutable about his look that was almost frightening. Wayne could almost hear the other's mind whirring in his head, trying to form some plan that would enable him to sneak away in the darkness, even if he didn't manage to get his hands on a gun. A few feet away, Kerrick seemed to be asleep, but in the darkness it was impossible to be sure. Hard to say which of the two was the more dangerous.

Yarrow snorted, rolled over on to his back. His breathing became more even again. The sight of him asleep only made Wayne want to close his eyes and surrender to his weariness all the more and the fact that he knew he dare not do it, mercly made it more difficult to fight against it. He glanced towards the east, looking for any sign of the dawn, but the darkness there was just as absolute as in any other direction.

Settling back on his elbows, he took out the makings of a cigarette, rolled the tobacco gently in the piece of brown paper, placed it between his lips and lit it, drawing the smoke deeply into his lungs. It irritated his parched throat but it served to keep him awake. Still Quentin had not moved. He might have been a man carved out of stone.

I'm just working on nerves and courage now, he thought to himself, and will these be enough when thirst and fatigue and hunger really start to bear down in the coming two days? It was one thing to have a reserve of strength when he was hunting down Quentin with two other men riding alongside him, but it was quite different now. Then the danger had been ahead of him. Now it was right here with him and could strike any moment his vigilance relaxed.

'Still awake, Everett?' Quentin's voice reached him softly from the darkness.

'You can bet on that,' he said harshly.

'And when it comes your turn, do you

think you can trust Yarrow to keep a good watch on us? Seems to me he don't have the same reasons you do for wantin' to turn us in. Reckon if I was to make it worth his while, he might reconsider whose side he's on. Five thousand dollars and the chance to slip away across the border just for turning his back for a couple of minutes. Ain't many men who could resist an offer like that, now are there?' The other paused and when Wayne said nothing, he went on: 'Oh, I know I'd just be wastin' my time makin' an offer like that to you. You've got principles and you'll stick by them even if they result in you dyin' for them. But men like Yarrow are shallow-minded. He'll jump at the offer and he knows I'm a man who keeps my word. I can pay him that much and never miss it.'

Wayne still said nothing, sat staring at the redly glowing tip of his cigarette. The spiralling cigarette smoke that curled up in front of his face laced painfully across his weary, red-rimmed eyes, but he gave no outward sign of it. This was a possibility which had already occurred to him. How far Yarrow could be trusted to keep faith with him and get these two back to Yuma, he did not know. Certainly, five thousand dollars would be far more than he could ever hope to lay his hands on honestly in his entire lifetime. Wayne's life would mean nothing to him if it came to such a showdown. Trouble was, that once they had dealt with him, Yarrow's life would not be worth a plugged nickel. He was a witness to what had happened and he could not be allowed to live so that he might testify.

He smoked the cigarette slowly, then flicked the glowing butt away, sending it spinning into the sand. He saw Quentin's head turn slowly to follow the crimson arc, then look back at him. Gingerly he touched his cheeks where the hot sun had scorched the flesh and the dust storm had rubbed them raw. There was a smear of dried blood there, encrusted on his skin. His head began to ache as if a tight band, like an encircling strip of metal had been coiled around his forehead and was slowly contracting against the flesh, squeezing inexorably. He tried vainly to ignore it, knew that it had to be some effect of the utter weariness, the need for sleep. A man could go without food for quite a while without any more ill effects than a gnawing ache in his belly; but if he tried to go without water and sleep, then it would show very soon. This had to be one of the first symptoms. He shook his head in an effort to rid it of the throbbing pain, but the movement only made it worse.

Over Quentin's head, he could see the moon, the merest crescent low on the eastern horizon. It must have risen un-noticed sometime during the past quarter of an hour or so. Now it was swaying gently, swinging from side to side in ever-increasing arcs. Blinking his eyes, he tried to right his vision, tried to tell himself that this was not really happening, it all existed only in his imagination, brought on by his physical condition. Maybe he ought to waken Yarrow and take an hour's sleep himself.

His head jerked to one side. The spasm of pain that shot through the muscles of his neck jarred him awake. He swallowed, stiffened as he realised that he must have dropped off. How long he had been asleep he did not know. Swiftly, every sense humming with that curiously enhanced wakefulness that usually comes at the end of a nightmare, he stared about him. Quentin was no longer seated directly opposite him.

Twisting around on the sand, his right hand flashed towards the gun at his waist. Even as his fingers clawed at the butt, he saw Quentin bent over Yarrow. The Connaught boss's arm was upraised and there was a length of wood in it, a club that he brought smashing down on to the back of the man's head. It struck home with a sickening sound. Dropping the wood, Quentin grabbed at Yarrow's gun, straightened catlike, whirled on Wayne. The twin gunshots came so close together that one was a mere echo of the other. Wayne felt the wind of the bullet as it flashed past his cheek and buried itself in the sand near his head. At the same instant, Quentin uttered a shrill cry of pain and anger, the Colt spinning from his hand. He clutched at his shattered wrist, holding it tightly with his other hand.

'Back off, Quentin,' Wayne said warningly.

The other took two steps back, moaning through his tightly-clenched teeth. 'God-damn you,' he snarled. 'You've broken my wrist.'

'You want to be thankful I didn't put that bullet through your head.' Wayne got to his feet, prodded Kerrick to his as the other stirred on the ground.

'Get up, Kerrick. Quentin wants you to bind up his wrist. Then we move out again and–'

He broke off sharply as the horses, spooked by the gunshots bucked and reared nearby. For a moment the grounded reins held, then they came loose. Seconds later, the four horses were galloping off into the darkness.

Even Quentin had stopped his moaning, staring after the fleeing animals. Wayne felt a sinking sensation of disaster in his mind. Without the horses it would be an almost impossible task to get through to Yuma. The only bright spot was that they had taken their canteens from the saddles and they were now lying in the sand nearby. But what use was half a canteen of water if they had to make it on foot across the desert?

With an effort, he pulled himself together. If they were to get out of this mess alive, they could afford to wait no longer. To Kerrick, he said: 'Tear a strip off Quentin's shirt and strap up his wrist. Then we move out.'

'Are you crazy!' Quentin's high-pitched voice held a curiously whining note. 'We don't stand a chance out there on foot.'

'If you can think of any other way of gettin' back to Yuma, then spit it out,' said Wayne sharply. 'If not, then we move out on foot.'

While he had been speaking, he had gone down on one knee beside Yarrow, turning the other over with his left hand, while he kept the Colt in his right hand trained on the two men. He felt for the pulse in the flaccid wrist, but there was nothing. Getting to his feet, he stared directly at Quentin. 'I reckon I've got a charge of murder here that I can make stick and no amount of fast talkin' is goin' to get you out of it.'

Kerrick finished binding up Quentin's smashed wrist and then they set out, Wayne walking a few feet behind the others. Two hours later, at daybreak, they halted. Ahead of them, the desert stretched for perhaps a mile to where the low range of hills lifted on the skyline, purple in the light of the brightening dawn. In order to preserve the small amount of water they had left, they did not drink, but merely moistened their lips and sucked a little of the dampness of the night from their shirts.

When they started out again with the hills to guide them, there was something deceptively pleasant and invigorating in the first hour after sun-up. The air was crystal clear and the terrible, blistering heat of the day had not yet had a chance to make itself felt. None of the dust lifted under their feet and they made better progress than Wayne had thought possible when they had first set out.

The desert was a pale yellow background, an almost perfect setting for the play of delicate pastel shades over the hills to the east where purples and blues shifted in a swirling of smooth hues. During that hour, Wayne felt a growing confidence. They were going to make it after all. There was shade in the hills and they could stay out of the glaring heat of the sun around high noon, pushing on in the late afternoon and through the coming night and by dawn the next day they ought to be somewhere close to Yuma.

An hour later, when they were still a quarter of a mile or so from the hills and the sun had lifted higher into the cloudless heavens, the heat had a bite to it and he knew that the day was going to be bad. He felt his earlier confidence wane. Stumbling, eyes smarting as the glare lanced painfully into them, with the heat refracted from the rocky outcrops that were becoming more numerous now, exhaustion laid its gripping fingers on them.

The hours became long, nightmare things, full of flame and heat. It was difficult to see properly. The two men in front of him were vague, indistinct shapes, in as bad a physical condition as he was, thrusting their shuffling feet through the sand that sloughed off their boots like water, burning through the soles of their feet until it seemed they were walking on a bed of hot coals.

Wayne could feel his legs growing stiff, rigid. His muscles had to be forced to obey his flagging will. He limped painfully and he had taken out the Colt from its holster, now walked with it clutched tightly in his right hand. His entire heat-ridden body felt on fire, the sweat running down his limbs, the glare fogging his vision more and more, sickness growing in the pit of his stomach, threatening to surge up and overwhelm him utterly. The craving for water, the urge to uncork the canteen and let all of the water there go splashing in a cooling, refreshing stream down his throat became unbearable.

8

THE MORENCI KID

Night brought no respite. The day had passed in a suffering of heat and pain. Both Quentin and Kerrick seemed to have given up any ideas they may have had about attempting to go for his gun. Movement was automatic, a shuffling gait. When the sun had finally slid beneath the western horizon, leaving a blood-red wake behind it and the heat of the day had dissipated, there had been a brief while, like that immediately following the dawn, when the air was cool and the world was a blue land, full of the smell of the hills about them. The bitter, scorched smell of the scant vegetation had given way to the scent of sage and bitter cacti. But the temperature had fallen swiftly with the coming of night and their sweat lay cold on their bodies, threatening to freeze the blood in their veins. Wayne found himself shivering convulsively as he plodded forward in the wake of the two men.

His lips were sore and cracked and the dust had worked its way into them so that they seemed swollen to twice their normal size. His mouth was thick with a foul fur which he could not spit out no matter how hard he tried. His feet were blistered on soles and heels.

Quentin halted abruptly, so quickly that Kerrick, walking with his head bowed, bumped into him, almost sending him sprawling.

'Keep moving,' Wayne said through swollen lips. His voice was now little more than a harsh croak, but there was a note of authority in it, backed up by the pistol in his hand.

'We've got to rest up,' muttered the other. 'This is sheer madness, trying to make it to Yuma like this. We don't stand a chance in hell. We'll all be dead long before we get there.'

'Then that's too bad on you,' Wayne said harshly. 'You got us into this mess by spookin' those horses last night. Now you're goin' to have to pay for your folly.'

'You can't make me go on movin'.'

'If you're hopin' we'll leave you so that on the chance that some of your men didn't desert you and ride clear to the border, they might find you before it's too late, then you're wrong. How long do you reckon you'd survive here if we took the rest of your water?'

'Aren't you takin' a lot for granted, Everett? You seem to forget that Kerrick here works for me. He knows what he can expect if he ever sets foot in Yuma again and he'll stick with me.'

Wayne threw a quick glance at the gunman, standing near by. His lips curled back in an expression of derision. 'You don't know the kind of man that Kerrick is,' he said flatly. 'He knows damned well that I don't have any murder charge hangin' over him as I do you. He's prepared to take his chances so long as he gets to Yuma alive. Ain't that so, Kerrick?'

For several moments, the other made no reply. Then he snarled viciously. 'All right, Everett. So you know a lot about me. But you're still just one man against two and you can't keep goin' like this much longer. You're almost out on your feet now. Another few hours and you'll drop.'

'I wouldn't make any bets on that. And you're forgetting that it's two against two. I've got this.' He made a threatening gesture with the Colt in his fist. 'Now step it out, Quentin, before I put a bullet in your leg and Kerrick here has to carry you the rest of the way.'

'You're bluffin',' said Quentin.

'Then why not call my bluff?' Wayne lowered the barrel of the pistol until it pointed at the other's leg, just above the kneecap. His finger tightened on the trigger. For a moment, the other remained standing defiantly. Then with a muttered curse he swung around and continued marching through the rocks.

By the time the eastern sky began to bleach, they had made their way down from the hills and were in the rolling desert once more. Wayne rubbed the back of his hand across his eyes. If they had come down from the hills anywhere near the main trail, he reckoned they were about five miles west of Yuma. He watched the sun rise dully through eyes that were now half closed from lack of sleep, red from the sand and the glare. His legs ached as if they had been lacerated with a thousand razor-edged knives, smeared with dust and blood. A spent body which kept moving because of some inner will that seemed entirely divorced from his tired mind.

He had heard somewhere that even when

it seemed that all of the strength and will had gone from the body, self-preservation proved a strong enough force to keep a man going after all else was gone. It was this now which they called upon to keep them going through the long day that stretched ahead of them, through long hours which seemed to have no end; heat-filled hours with only the slow-wheeling buzzards above them to keep them company through the desert.

High noon came and went in an eye-searing haze, the burning heat rolling down on them like a suffocating blanket that burned all of the colour out of the ground around them, that sickened them through and through, threatened to blind them. By afternoon, they were scarcely able to stagger forward. The gun in Wayne's hand seemed to weigh a ton. Staring down at the piece of metal, the lances of brilliance that the sun struck from it glancing painfully into his sand-encrusted eyes, he tried to think why he was carrying it. There had to be some reason why it was there, but his dulled mind seemed unable to comprehend it.

Sucking a gust of heat-laden air into his lungs, he lifted his head and peered off into the distance. The plain shimmered in front of him. The skyline tilted from one side to the other as if the Earth itself was moving on its axis. There was a dark smudge on the skyline a little to their left. Wayne stared at it numbly. He did not know when he had become aware of it, nor how long he had been looking at it before the realisation of what it was penetrated his dulled mind.

Yuma! It had to be; there was nothing else that it could be. With an effort, he forced his flagging footsteps to lengthen their stride through the sand that shifted under him like water.

An hour later, incredibly, they were in the main street of the town. Wayne straightened himself perceptibly. His clothing still felt clammy with sweat and he knew he looked a sight, but he forced himself to stay upright as he made his way towards the sheriff's office.

A few people on the boardwalks stopped and stared at the trio. Wayne made the two men go in first, followed them quickly inside. Luke Paine was seated behind his desk, feet up, when they entered. For a moment, he stared open-mouthed, first at Quentin and then at Wayne, noticing the gun the other held in his hand. Thrusting his feet to the floor, he got up, demanded harshly: 'What the thunderin' tarnation is the meanin' of this, Everett? You taken leave of your senses?'

'Not quite, Sheriff,' Wayne said grimly. 'I want these two men locked up until they can be brought to trial.'

'On what charge?'

'Murder against Quentin. As for Kerrick here, I figure we can get somethin' which will stick against him. If we don't know anythin', a message through to Los Lobos, to the sheriff there will get somethin'.'

'Are you plain loco?' Paine's brow puckered in sudden consternation. He stared at Quentin appealingly.

'Sure he is,' said Quentin quickly, the words spilling over each other as he blurted them out. 'Don't listen to a word he says, Paine. I put you where you are now and I want him arrested for attempted murder. He jumped Kerrick and myself out in the desert, ran off the horses, then forced us to get back here on foot.'

'You're talkin' yourself right into a noose, Quentin,' Wayne said. 'If I'd done what you said, the last thing I'd do then would be to drag you back here to Yuma to talk about it. I'd have shot you out there in the desert and made it clear to the border.' He saw the look of indecision on Paine's face, went on deliberately, 'Quentin and his men left Yuma nearly a week ago to destroy the Overland wagon train headin' for the Army outposts with the supplies they picked up under that military contract that Mary Vender beat Quentin to the punch with; and they nearly made it. Trouble was, they hadn't reckoned on the Overland teamsters puttin' up a fight. That freight train has gone through and in a week or so, they'll be back with enough proof to hang Quentin, and probably his sidekick here, too. Guess you wouldn't want to buck the Army by not takin' action here in Yuma, Paine.'

'Sure, but–' The other hesitated, then went over to the wall behind his desk, took down the bunch of keys and motioned towards the door at the far side of the office.

'You'll regret this, Paine, I assure you,' snarled Quentin as he moved ahead of the other.

As Kerrick made to follow also, Wayne said sharply. 'Not you, Kerrick. There are one or two questions I want to ask you.'

The other's chin was close to his chest, but he was watching Wayne and he did not answer. Paine looked at Wayne curiously for a moment, then shrugged, went after Quentin. A few moments later there was the dull

232

metallic clang of a cell door closing and Paine came back. He seemed to be an exceedingly worried man.

Wayne said. 'Relax, Sheriff. You look like a man with all the worries of the world resting on his shoulders. Kerrick here is goin' to tell us about the plans Quentin made, so you'll know exactly where you stand.'

'I'm sayin' nothing,' muttered the gunman harshly. Wayne holstered his gun and stepped closer. 'Quentin hired you in Los Lobos, paid you to ride into town on the stage and act the part of the Morenci Kid. Now why would he want to do that?'

'Your guess is as good as mine,' muttered the other sullenly. 'If you want to know any more why don't you go in there and ask him yourself?'

'Because I prefer you to tell me. Now once more, why were you hired to impersonate the Morenci Kid?'

'Give me a drink of water. I'm dying of thirst and–' He was saying it as Wayne drew back his fist and hit him. The other's head snapped back on his shoulders and he would have fallen to the floor had not the edge of the desk caught him in the middle of the back. He swayed, came slowly upright, eyes glinting dangerously. Gently, he fingered his cheek and then his eyes came full awake.

'When I ask you a question, punk, you answer it.'

'All right. No need to start gettin' rough. He said he'd sent a message to the Morenci Kid to ride into Yuma and get rid of some *hombres* who were stoppin' him from buyin' out some freighting outfit.'

'The Overland Company?'

'That's the one. He said the Morenci Kid hadn't turned up. My guess is that he was yeller. But he made me a good offer, said there'd be no real trouble, that he had everythin' sewn up real tight here and that there was only a woman standin' out against him.'

'And you figured that it would be an easy thing to scare a woman out.'

'Made little difference to me who it was,' mumbled the other. 'The money he offered was as good as any I've made, so I took it.'

'And it was Quentin's idea to follow the Overland wagon train and destroy it before it could reach the Army outposts and deliver those supplies.'

The other hesitated, saw Wayne's upraised fist cocked to strike again and nodded quickly, swallowing. 'That's right. He tried to get that Army contract himself. But when they gave it to the Overland, he sent his men after the train. They had orders just to kill ever man riding with it. He wanted the wagons and the supplies intact if he could get his hands on them.'

'But he was quite prepared to destroy them utterly if that was only way he could stop them?'

'I guess so. He didn't tell me everythin' he meant to do.'

Wayne's lips curled derisively. 'I can't say I blame him for that much anyway.' Moving over to the desk, he sat on the edge, one leg swinging idly. Then he glanced at the sheriff. 'Heard enough?' he asked.

The other nodded his head slowly. 'I guess you've got enough on them to have them held in jail until the wagon train gets back. The circuit judge won't be here for another couple of weeks yet.'

'Then lock him up and see that they're not in the same cell. I wouldn't trust either of them as far as I could throw my hat.'

Wayne waited until Kerrick had been locked in one of the cells, then made his way out into the street. The deep-seated weariness that was in him was making itself felt now. During the past few minutes, inside the sheriff's office, he had been able to forget about it for a little while. But now all he wanted to do was get a long, cool beer, something to eat and then a hot bath. After that he meant to get himself a bed and sleep the clock around.

Stepping down into the dusty street, he walked slowly to the far side, towards the saloon. He was halfway there when he heard the running steps behind him and a moment later, he turned to see Mary Vender hurrying towards him. There was a look of deep concern written on her face as she caught at his arm.

'Wayne! Oh, my God, what happened?'

'It's a long story,' he mumbled. God, what a sight he must look to her. 'I was just goin' inside for a beer and–'

'I've got beer at the office,' she said, steering him along the street. 'There's no need to go in there for it.'

'I make it a rule never to drink on the premises where I work,' he said dully.

'This time you will,' she said firmly. She took his weight against her side as he swayed and would have fallen. Inside the Overland offices, after helping him up the wooden steps, she led him to a chair, watched for a moment as he lay there, utterly spent. Then she poured out the glass of beer and handed it to him.

'Drink this,' she said softly. 'Then sleep if you want to.'

'But I can't–' he began.

'Hush,' she said softly. 'You're all right now.' She put her hand against his chest as he struggled to rise. He dropped back into the wide chair, legs thrust out in front of him. The beer was cool and cleansing in his mouth. When it was finished, he lay on his back, his eyes closed. He was aware of her presence in the room nearby, but he seemed to lack the strength to open his eyes and see what she was doing.

'You must have been through hell to get like this,' she said, her voice a low, husky murmur.

'I guess you're right,' he muttered.

She did not say anything for a while after that but merely stood looking down at him and there was now a tenderness on her face and in her mind which she could not remember ever feeling for anyone since the day her father had died. Presently, he opened his eyes slowly, looked up to see her standing over him, her eyes darkly mysterious. The sunlight lancing through the street window touched her face with shadow and made a pale halo of her hair where it framed her face and fell in soft waves to her shoulders. Her thoughts were of him and it showed clearly in her eyes and in the soft contours of her face. 'Sleep now,' she said gently. 'You'll feel better when you wake. Then there'll be time to tell me what happened.'

'A long story,' he mumbled. He closed his eyes again, felt himself sinking down into a soft, deep darkness. For several moments, she stood there in the sunlight watching him. His regular breathing told her he was asleep. In a gentle whisper, she murmured, 'You're a strange man, Wayne. I've never known anyone who could affect me in this way.' His breathing was still even and she knew that he had not heard. Bending, she pulled off the boots, dusted and streaked with sand, set them on one side. In sleep, she noticed, a lot of the hardness went out of his face and even through the dirt and grime, the six day's growth of beard on his chin, she saw that it was a deeply sensitive face, not that of an outlaw or killer as she had first thought him to be. Yet there was ruthlessness there, too, a faint hint of a singleness of purpose that could make him a dangerous man if he so chose.

She stayed there for several minutes longer, then tiptoed out. On the steps she met Carmody.

'Wayne is back,' she said in a low voice. 'He's asleep in there. I want you to keep an eye on him. See that nobody disturbs him and let me know the minute he wakes. It isn't to be for some hours yet.'

'I'll do that,' nodded the other. He went into the office and closed the door gently behind him.

Sometime, hours later, Wayne woke briefly at a sudden sound that reached down into his unconscious mind, a sharp sound with an echo to it. But it was like a sound heard in a dream and rolling over on to his side, he fell asleep again. When he next woke, it was dark outside. Pushing himself up on his arms, he stared about him, not comprehending where he was for several moments. Then he noticed the furniture in the small room, saw his feet sticking out on the floor in front of him, from under the heavy rug which had been thrown over him, and remembered the events of the previous day when he had been brought here by Mary Vender.

How long had he been asleep, he wondered? He judged that it was sometime shortly before dawn. Getting stiffly to his feet he went over to the window and peered out. There was a faintly seen streaking of grey low in the east, with the roofs of the buildings on the edge of town just showing in silhouette against it. Stretching, he rubbed his face, felt the thick stubble there, recalled that he had neither washed nor shaved when he had arrived in town. He went back to the chair, sat down and put on his boots. His limbs were stiff, but otherwise he felt fine, his mind crystal clear, ready for anything. When he went over and tried the door, he found that it was locked.

Shrugging, he went back to the chair and stretched himself out in it once more, tried to compose his thoughts, get them into some kind of order. He had brought Quentin in for trial as he had sworn he would. But he had the feeling that things were not going to be quite as easy as that. The other undoubtedly had powerful friends here in Yuma. He was on his own home territory and there would almost certainly be some attempt made to bail him out of prison. Knowing Paine, it was doubtful if the other would do much to hold him in jail.

Maybe if he was to have a word with the Army commander, Colonel Parker – but the other would want proof of some kind and even then it was possible that Parker would feel unable to step in, probably insisting that this was a matter for the duly elected sheriff.

Sighing, he waited for the dawn. Almost exactly at sunup, he heard the steps on the stairs outside and a moment later, a key turned in the lock and the diminutive clerk came in.

'Glad to see you're up, Mister Everett,' he said respectfully. 'I trust you had a good night's sleep. You were so deeply asleep when I left last night, I decided to leave you here. I hope you don't mind?'

'Not at all.' Wayne got to his feet. 'I don't suppose you'd have such a thing as a razor and some hot water.'

'I'll get one of the boys to fetch one for you.' The other hurried to the door. 'There'll be hot water in ten minutes.'

Wayne shaved ten minutes later in front of the small, cracked mirror hanging from the crooked nail in the wall by the door. He had just finished making himself presentable when Mary came in. For a moment, seeing her standing there, the warm feeling came flooding back to him, a feeling he thought he had forgotten over the years, the sense of exhilaration, of believing that everything in the world was good and fresh and new. Then he remembered Quentin, in jail, and that took the edge off the pleasant feeling and left him with the nagging worries that ate at the edges of his mind, giving him a sense of emptiness in his stomach.

'You look a lot better than you did yesterday,' she said brightly. She smiled warmly at him, took off her bonnet, shook her head so that the hair fell in glowing cascades around her neck.

'I feel a lot better,' he told her. He paused, then went on: 'You asked me yesterday what happened out there on the trail. I think I'd better tell you and then–'

'You can tell me just as well over breakfast,' she said, stopping his flow of words.

Fifteen minutes later, they were seated at a table in the small diner along the street. Over the meal, he told her all that had happened, since he had ridden out of town with Slim and Yarrow, of the attack on the wagon train, Yarrow's death in the desert and the nightmare journey back to Yuma with his two prisoners.

The girl listened to him in silence. When he had finished, she said: 'I guessed that was what might perhaps happen when I sent the men out. I'm only glad it didn't turn out quite as bad as I had feared. And you say the wagon train is on its way to the outposts.'

'They had less water than they really needed, but I figure they'd get through all right.'

'And Quentin's men?'

He grinned, shook his head as he drained his coffee cup and filled it up for a second time. 'There will be no more trouble from them. They're scattered by now. Once the man they follow fails to go through with somethin' and shows that he isn't the leader they figured he was, they desert him. He's finished now and I reckon he knows it. He's no longer a menace in this territory and when the circuit judge gets here, I figure that—'

'Wayne.' She spoke in a thin little voice, watching his face closely. She had something to tell him and the telling of it was not easy. 'Something happened during the night. Just after midnight. Sheriff Paine must have had second thoughts about Quentin and this gunman. He let them out of their cells. One of them, we don't yet know who it was, must have grabbed his gun and shot him in the back. He's in the mortuary now.'

Wayne sat wholly still as she told him this, lips stretched thin over his teeth. His eyes changed and a deep anger stirred in their depths. 'And where are they now?' he asked in a harsh whisper. 'Does anyone know?'

'I think they're still in town. Quentin was heard to say that he meant to fix you before he did anything else. I think this gunfighter is with him.'

Wayne let his breath go in a long sigh. Perhaps he should have foreseen this and taken steps to ensure that it did not happen, he thought tightly. After all that he had gone through to bring them in, they had escaped as easily as this. Certainly Paine had paid the penalty of his stupidity. But that did not alter matters. Somewhere in the town, Quentin and Kerrick were lying in wait for him, biding their time, waiting for their opportunity to shoot him down from ambush; and they both knew he would have to go out after them. He had no other choice now.

'What are you going to do, Wayne?'

'There's only one thing I can do. I've got to go out and get them.'

Across the table, her eyes begged him to change his mind; but inwardly she knew he would not, that nothing could swerve him from this decision now. He took in his breath, let it out softly.

'If you're determined to go through with this, maybe I can get some men to help you and–'

'No, Mary.' His tone was firm, brooked of no argument. 'This is a chore I have to do myself.'

'Be careful, Wayne,' she said in a low whisper.

'I will.' His tone was soft. Reaching forward, he placed his hand over hers on the table. 'Mary, I know I've got no right to ask this, but–'

Her smile was soft and warm. 'I know what it is you're trying to say – and the answer is yes.'

For a moment, his fingers tightened on hers. Then he said: 'I hope you'll remember this, Mary. No matter what happens.'

'I will.'

For a moment he sat there, then he scraped back his chair, got to his feet, hitched up the gunbelt around his waist. Outside in the street, he paused to throw a quick glance up and down it. Sunlight had reached the town, it filtered along the main street and into the narrow alleys that opened off from it on both sides. It glowed on the cracked, painted signs that swung outside the saloons and stores. Making his way across the street, he pushed open the doors of the saloon. Errol, standing behind the bar, glanced up.

Wayne called: 'Have Quentin or that

gunslingin' sidekick of his been in here this mornin', Flint?'

'Haven't seen either of 'em, Wayne,' called the other.

'Thanks.' He stepped down into the street again. There was a deep blanket of silence hanging over the town which he had noticed almost at once; it had a peculiar waiting quality to it that he found oddly disturbing. Keeping to the middle of the wide street, he walked slowly along it, every nerve tensed, his gaze flickering from side to side. A dog dragged itself out of a pool of warm sunlight into a shadow, lay there panting. Halfway along the street one of the storekeepers brushed some of the litter out of the shop across the boardwalk and into the dust. He looked up at Wayne, recognised him and something in his stance must have touched a chord deep within him for he backed swiftly into the shop and slammed the door.

Stillness, deep and tangible, closed in on him from all sides. As far as he could see, the street was deserted. He glanced into each alley as he drew level with it, his nerves stretched taut within him. Had the two men decided that caution and prudence was the better part of valour and fled the town. Maybe at that very moment, they were riding hell for leather to the Mexico border, south of Yuma, taking with them all the money they could lay their hands on.

Scarcely had the thought crossed his mind, than a movement in the alley to his right snapped Wayne's attention to it. A moment later, Kerrick stepped out into the street. There was a vicious, thin-lipped grin on his face. He moved to the middle of the street, then stood there, staring at Wayne out of empty eyes. Wayne noticed that the other had placed himself so that the sunlight was in his eyes.

'That's far enough, Everett,' Kerrick called harshly. 'I've been waitin' for this. Now that we're on even terms, we'll see just what you can do when you come up against a seasoned gunman. Got any last requests you'd like to make?'

Wayne stood quite still. He felt certain that this was a trap; unless the other felt so confident of his ability to beat him to the draw in a fair fight and was challenging him there and then.

'Where's Quentin?' he called. 'Hidin' in the shadows some place with a rifle laid on my back?'

'I'm right here, Everett.'

Out of the corner of his eye, Wayne saw

Quentin step into view on the edge of the boardwalk to his right. He noticed that the other was wearing a gun, but he deliberately kept his hands well away from his sides, leaning almost nonchalantly against one of the wooden uprights.

'I don't need anybody to back my play, Everett,' said Kerrick harshly.

'That's right.' There was a heavy beat of sarcastic triumph in Quentin's voice. 'I brought Kerrick here to take care of things for me in Yuma. This has happened a little later than I'd hoped, and you were the cause of the delay yourself, so it's only justice I reckon that he should kill you here and now.'

'If he thinks he can,' said Wayne deliberately. 'Seems to me that he's been all talk in the past. Could be he's gettin' set to talk me to death, too.'

There was no reply from Kerrick. He smiled thin-lipped at Wayne, his eyes cold and empty. His hands were close to the guns at his waist, his body crouched forward a little in the usual gunhawk's stance, holding himself so that he did not have so far to reach for the handles of the Colts.

Vaguely, Wayne was aware of the presence of some of the other citizens of Yuma on the boardwalks, keeping well out of the line of fire. Kerrick moved a couple of paces forward, then stopped.

'This is where you get it, cowboy,' he said deliberately.

'You've got your blood money from Quentin,' Wayne said quietly. 'Now let's see if you can earn it.' The insult in his voice was not lost on the other. He saw the faint flush that rose to the man's face, then the other struck down for his guns. He was devil fast, his hands moving in a blur of speed. The guns seemed to leap into his hands of their own accord, but the first shots came from the heavy Colt in Wayne's hand, two shots triggered off so rapidly that they blurred into a single smash of sound, echoes bounding off the walls of the buildings along the street. The guns in Kerrick's hands roared once as he teetered forward, knees sagging under him. A look of stupefied amazement spread over his face as he went down. The slugs from his guns ploughed into the dust a couple of yards in front of his body as he crashed forward on to his face and lay still in the dust.

There was a moment of silence, then Quentin snatched at his guns. Swinging, Wayne fired once. The bullet took Quentin in the chest. For a moment, he remained upright, the Colts slipping from his hands, crashing into the dust at his feet. Clutching at the post with both hands as he went down, he lay sprawled in the dirt, features twisted into a grimace of pain. For a moment he held life in his eyes as the blood soaked into his gaudy shirt. His lips worked convulsively as he tried to speak.

At first, only a vague muttering came from his lips, then he said in a hoarse, bubbling tone, 'Too fast, even for Kerrick. Who – who are you really, Everett?'

There was a faint smile on the other's face as he holstered the smoking Colt and walked slowly forward. He stared pitilessly down at the dying man's face, then said calmly, 'I'm the Morenci Kid, Quentin.'

The two bodies had been carried into the mortuary to lie alongside that of Sheriff Luke Paine and Wayne made his way slowly back to the Overland offices. When he got to them he saw Mary standing at the top of the steps waiting for him. He made his way slowly up the stairs, stopped at the top and looked at her. 'It's all finished,' he said simply.

'And the Morenci Kid,' she murmured;

not removing her gaze from his face. 'Can he fade into oblivion with them, too?'

He returned her steady gaze, said: 'How long have you known?'

'For a long time, I think. There was something about you I couldn't fathom. A sureness you had, I think, or maybe more than that.'

'And it makes no difference to you?'

'Why should it? The stories they tell about you. How many are true? Fast with a gun, but that doesn't always turn a man into an outlaw. I knew there were depths in you that maybe you hadn't even plumbed. I've seen you when you're asleep and everything on the surface is washed away then and one sees only the part that really matters.'

He looked at her in silence for a long time, thinking things that had been suppressed in his mind for a long time, for an eternity it seemed. He saw the look on her face, the shoulders, the shape of her and again there came that burst of sunwarmth which engulfed him almost completely to the exclusion of all else.

'You won't be riding on now, will you?' she asked softly. He shook his head. She did not move away at the pressure of his hands on her shoulders. He pulled her to him, felt the warmth, the sweetness of her, knew there had never been anything like this before in his life.

Her lips trembled just a little and as he kissed her, he remembered what Quentin had said that night on the trail, that she lacked warmth and would only marry a man for his money, for nothing else. How wrong could any man be, he thought briefly as the warmth came out and engulfed him?

When he finally released her, she said: 'It was hard not to come to you before, Wayne. But there are things that a man has to do and a woman cannot step between him and them. She must wait until he's done everything that has to be done and then, if he still wants her she will be waiting.'

'There's been a lot of trouble and misery,' he said soberly.

She nodded. 'I felt that when my father was killed. It was as if the end of the world had come and there was nothing left to go on living for. But time heals all things, makes us realise that there can be good, beautiful things in the world if we're prepared to look and wait for them.' She opened the door and went inside.

'With Quentin finished, there will be a lot to do in Yuma. The freight line will have to

252

be built up and although I've done my best with it over the past few months, it needs a man's touch. This frontier is good. It's going to be a great place one of these days once we can rid ourselves of the evil and the corruption.'

The way she said it struck him more powerfully than anything he had ever known. He walked over to the window and stood beside her, looking down. The sun was high now, climbing swiftly up the sky in the south-east. It flooded warmly, yellowly, over the whole of the town spread out beneath them. Off in the distance, the wide river glinted in the sunlight.

The faint wail of a siren reached them over the roof tops. More ships would be making their way up from the Gulf of California, docking at the quayside, unloading their cargos. Sometime, he thought to himself, there would be better and faster methods of shifting them to the different parts of this great country, but until that happened, they would have to rely on the ships and the great freight wagons, moving along the endless trails of the desert.

The publishers hope that this book has given you enjoyable reading. Large Print Books are especially designed to be as easy to see and hold as possible. If you wish a complete list of our books please ask at your local library or write directly to:

Dales Large Print Books
Magna House, Long Preston,
Skipton, North Yorkshire.
BD23 4ND